Darkening 1

The Darkening of the Light
Or Life is But a Dream

By Tessa B. Dick

Cover art by Nick Buchanan

Dedication: *To Phil – my lover, my friend, my inspiration.*

Second edition, 2012
Create Space

New material has been added to this second
edition, which is an expanded version of an
earlier work by the same author.

Chapter One

You don't always get what you want, but sometimes a miracle occurs. Be careful what you ask for.

". . . however complex the object may be, the thought of it is one undivided state of consciousness."
(William James)

Action at a distance, as explained in the Einstein-Podolsky- Rosen Paradox, is possible because the external world exists only within the human mind.

This might not be the best of all possible worlds, but it is one of the worlds which nature prefers.

#

"Clear!" the doctor shouted, and then came the shock. Again he shouted, "Clear!" and again the shock came. And yet a third time, the charm, "Clear!" and then the shock, as if Dr. Frankenstein were bringing the monster to life. The dead parts began to live, and the sinus rhythm settled into a regular pattern on the monitor, and the beeping became more regular and less frantic.

Clearly the light had begun to darken, yet she lived. Unable to move, but seeing and hearing all those around her, she lay in the hospital bed while her faithful suitor sat in the chair and talked to her, or Mother sat reading aloud from the newspaper, even reading the want ads, but never the obituaries, for the thought of death must never enter this room.

Edna saw a raccoon climbing in through the window. Raccoons used to sneak into the kitchen at night and eat the cat food. Mom had the cat door removed, and Tuffy had to come in at night, so the coyotes wouldn't eat him. The raccoon dissolved and became a mere shadow, then was gone.

She began to remember how she had gotten to this place, to this state of being, and she began to see the raccoon everywhere, prowling through the hospital room, climbing the walls, opening cupboards and closets, hiding under the bed whenever a white-coated staff member came into the room.

#

Edna Eileen Stax gave her handbag to her mother and bravely lay down on the hospital bed where the nurses would prep her for the surgery. As a school teacher, she had risen to the top of the list for the new implant, and as the daughter of a wealthy family, she could afford to pay for it. She felt frightened and excited at the same time, anticipating the joy of having a wealth of information at her fingertips – or, more properly, at any wireless access terminal. She had no way of knowing that one of the nurses had failed to wash his hands before he helped with the shaving of her long blonde hair on the back of her neck, or that he had just come from assisting another patient with a bedpan.

Lying on her stomach with her head resting on a donut-shaped pillow, she allowed the operating room technicians to stabilize her head in a metal contraption that might have served as a tool of torture in another era. The poke of the needle stung when the anesthesiologist began numbing the back of her head, and she cried out.

"Sorry," she said. "You have a lot of nerves there on your scalp, but soon it will be numb." The anesthesiologist continued poking around with the needle, meticulously describing a circular pattern of shots around the surgical area. The needle stung every time, and the medicine burned as it went in.

Edna felt a sense of unreality in the operating room, where she was surrounded by masked people in green cotton suits, with plastic covers over their shoes and plastic gloves on their hands. The bright overhead lights washed out the little color that she could see in the stark white room. She had enjoyed good health all her life, aside from the usual childhood diseases, so to her mind the scene was like something from a soap opera, not real life.

Soon she felt nothing on the back of her head, and she tried to recall happy memories to relieve the sheer boredom. She could hear the snipping of scissors and the slicing of a scalpel, but she couldn't feel anything. The chip settled neatly into the base of her skull while nanotubes reached into her brain, connecting the chip to the relevant neurons. Edna had read all about the procedure, which was still quite experimental, and the surgical team had carefully explained it to her.

Thus, the only surprise in the actual experience was how much time it seemed to be taking. She felt nothing from the nanotubes, since the brain did not have tactile receptors, and she couldn't feel the cutting or the insertion of the chip because they had numbed her scalp with drugs. Even so, she wished that they had put her under for the procedure. It took so much time, and she had so many itches that she dared not scratch, especially the one of the back of her right thigh, the itch that she always got when she felt nervous.

Time, she had read in a book at the college library, is an illusion. It is a mental construct that enables us to make sense out of the relative motion between objects, the course of our lives and the inevitable entropy that will lead to the heat death of the universe in a homogeneity of cold. Or something like that; she knew that her mind had changed the words over time, memory being fungible at best. She tried to meditate and make the long time seem short.

#

Over the following weeks, Edna went to the university every day for two-hour sessions of testing and training, which took up most of the day because of the long drive from Yountville to the Bay and the time spent waiting in a nondescript room with months-old magazines and little else to occupy her mind. Her mother did the driving, insisting that she must rest and recuperate from her "major" surgery. Edna secretly enjoyed the extra attention, although she complained loudly. After all, she was twenty-two years old and had a job and her own money. And her own apartment, even though Mother had insisted that she come "home" and stay in her old bedroom for at least a few weeks.

She rather enjoyed squeezing into her old room, a twelve-by-twelve cubicle with a small bed against one wall and a small writing desk against another. *At least*, she thought with a smile, *Mom doesn't make me wear my old school clothes.* She had gone through high school wearing skirts so long that they covered her knees, with socks that came almost up to her knees and blouses that covered her neck all the way to her chin. The skirts were wool, no matter the season or the weather, and the tops of her blouses had bows that tied and felt like nooses around her neck. As a teacher, she wore equally modest clothing, but the knee socks and been replaced by nylon stockings and the skirts and blouses by stylish dresses and sometimes pants suits.

The old ranch-style mansion had a kitchen large enough to hold her entire apartment, and it used to have Fritz, who could and would prepare the most delicious meals. Of all the childhood memories that filled her mind when she came back home, the most vivid and pleasant were the hours she had spent sitting at the kitchen table and watching Fritz cook. Sometimes he even let her help.

She dreamed of sitting at the kitchen table, munching on a cinnamon roll while she watched Fritz expertly flip pancakes and strips of bacon. He coddled eggs in the water bath, too. The cinnamon soothed her tongue, but the aroma of breakfast made her stomach churn with anticipation. Then she saw the raccoon again, shambling across the slippery tiles of the kitchen floor with its peculiar gait. Raccoons have long legs and short arms, so they look like little kangaroos with long, striped tails when they walk on all fours.

Fritz had long since gone, retired to some family somewhere, Mom wasn't sure where. Edna's brothers had gone off to college and taken executive positions at big corporations back east, leaving the mansion hollow. Only the echoes of their childhood remained. Dad worked in the City, staying in a hotel during the week and coming home for weekend visits.

Hired hands tended the rows of grape vines that stood on either side of the long drive leading from the main road to their front door, cabernet and Riesling grape vines kept growing as a reminder of their beginnings, their literal and figurative roots. A small stucco building by the main road still proclaimed the Stax Winery with a fashionable wooden sign, and they offered wine tastings every Saturday afternoon. But the family money came mostly from the careful investment of inherited wealth, plus the generous salaries that they earned in business. Edna was expected to marry into money, her parents viewing her teaching career as a mere speed bump along the way to finding a proper husband.

She leaned back against the soft headrest on the passenger seat of Mom's Mercedes, watching the rows of grapes go by. The vines, held up by stakes and wires, hung heavy with purple grapes and green, the fruit of several generations of the Stax family. When they turned onto the main road, they passed through the shade of trees arching overhead, past the small white wooden buildings of what passed for a town in the Napa Valley, and then between pastures where cattle grazed. By the time they reached the freeway, Edna had fallen asleep to the notes of Beethoven's *Moonlight*, a sonata that Mom had taught her to play on the piano.

Mom had once nursed aspirations of becoming a classical musician, but then she had married Dad and settled into the role of a wife and mother, plus a notable figure in the community, especially with regard to charitable functions. Edna grew to love the upright grand piano that dominated one wall of the sitting room, but her stubby fingers prevented her from mastering the keys. She could barely reach across one octave, and even that was a stretch.

The testing sessions alternately puzzled her and bored her, the doctors showing her cards that she was supposed to organize so that they told a story, asking her to identify colors and shapes, numbers and letters, all presented not on the table in front of her, but through the chip in the base of her skull.

"What was that?" she asked, startled by a shadow of movement in the far corner of the testing room.

The professor turned, looked and said, "I don't see anything.

But the shadow returned. She said nothing, since it must be nothing. She suspected that it must be the raccoon.

Edna couldn't wait for September, when she could actually use her new mental tools in the classroom. Her third-graders would surely be impressed. In the meantime, she pretended that the stark white conference room with the long brown table and uncomfortable chairs where they trained and tested her was just another classroom. The chip was working within acceptable parameters, the team leader said, so she entered and left each day's session with a modicum of confidence beneath the nervous tension.

The raccoon made her nervous. It had begin to work mischief, shredding paper and urinating on it. At first it left the nasty mess in a corner of the testing room, but then it became more bold, plopping wads and shreds of paper under the testing table and urinating on them just inches from her feet. She didn't say anything to the others, because she knew that they would say she was hallucinating. The last thing she wanted was to have the chip removed or, worse, to be locked up in a mental ward.

She felt a great sense of relief when the car pulled into the drive and she was almost home. The daily testing recalled the anxiety of her college days, when each test filled her with anxiety. Pop quizzes were the worst, since she had no opportunity to prepare for them. She understood and sympathized with her third-graders, but testing was required as a part of the curriculum. She did her best to soften their anxiety, reminding them that this was an opportunity to show her what they knew, not a chance for her to find out what they didn't know. And she graded their papers with a purple pen, not the dreaded red ink.

She settled into a chair in the sitting room and began reading a book of Shakespeare's sonnets, while Mom instructed the new cook, Margie, to prepare dinner. They ate promptly at eight o'clock every evening. Mom considered punctuality a sign of good character, and she had a schedule for everything, every day. Mom never strolled through the patio or the flower garden unless such a stroll was written in her daybook. She never lingered there past the time when her schedule called for her to read the newspaper or make a phone call.

Mom used to screen Edna's calls and approve or, more often, disapprove the boys who wanted to take her out. She controlled every detail of her life. Boys were allowed to call between four and six, not a minute sooner or later, and if a call should go past six, she would hang up the phone and send Edna to her room to do homework. She understood that her mother loved her, but she had longed for the freedom to just be, without time controlling her every activity. *Time*, she mused, *ought to be spent, wasted and passed, without the rigor of a set schedule.*

Mom still controlled the land line in her house, but when Robert Wells called Edna's cell phone, Mom was bypassed. She had met him when she wandered into a record store in Berkley, looking for some music to play while she graded papers. She had already spent most of the day at the library, so evening was darkening the sky when she happened to notice the sign for Tower Records. Rob had been so attentive, and his eyes had sparkled so penetratingly, that she knew that he was up to something more than selling her a few CDs. "Do you live around here?" he asked. "I've never seen you before, and I would have remembered someone like you."

"Not really," she answered. "I go to the university."

The small talk continued while he helped her find Beethoven and Mozart, Bach and Scarlatti, all the music that could fill her tiny apartment with warm sound while she sat at the kitchen table grading papers. Although she was not in the habit of picking up strange men, when he asked her out she found herself saying yes.

"My shift ends in ten minutes," Rob said. "There's a nice café just down the street. Can I buy you a cup of coffee?"

The invitation seemed harmless enough, and so she found herself sitting in a dark corner of a small café with a man she had just met, and met by accident, laughing and smiling while discussing the details of their lives. She liked the way Robert's black hair kept falling over his brow, refusing to stay combed into order. His eyes, piercing blue eyes, seemed to look inside her, all the way to her soul. His voice, a pleasant tenor, rolled out like the notes of a popular song.

"My mother," he said, "wanted me to get a real job. You know, in an office somewhere with a good salary and benefits. Not a clerk's job in a record store."

"Why did you choose the job you have?" she asked.

"I love music."

"Me too." And then she told him about the piano and her stubby fingers, and about the family pressure to get married when all she wanted to do was teach children how to read, write and do arithmetic.

"Do you want children of your own?"

She laughed, throwing her head back, causing her long blonde curls to flutter like the wings of a bird struggling to take flight. "I would have to get married, then, wouldn't I?"

"Well, in this day and age, maybe not." He grinned.

"My parents would disown me." They would probably disown her anyway, if she married Robert, since he was neither wealthy nor prominent. And yet she knew, in that moment, that she was going to marry Robert Wells and bear his children. They dated off and on through the school year, growing closer and even kissing – only kissing, nothing more.

When he came to the door of her parents' mansion, Edna was already waiting to open it for him. She resolved not to let Mom interfere. "I'll see you later," she called.

"Where are you going?" Mom's voice approached the foyer with hurried footsteps.

"Out. Robert is taking me out to dinner. Don't wait up for me." But she knew that Mom would be sitting up, waiting, when she got home.

#

Robert sped through the streets of the unfamiliar city, keeping one eye on the GPS on the dashboard of his Chevy Malibu, heading to the nearest hospital. Edna, his sweet Edna, needed help. NOW. They had been making small talk, laughing and smiling, when suddenly her head fell forward and her whole body shook, and then her limbs flailed. The seat belt and shoulder strap held her in place, but she fell like an old sweater tossed aside, and then she became horrifyingly still.

He drove right up to the double glass doors of the emergency room, opened the passenger door, undid the seatbelt and lifted Edna's limp body into his arms. Running through the automatic doors, he nearly crashed into them while they slid to the side. "Help!" he shouted. "We need help!"

He sat in the waiting room for hours after they took Edna into some back room. A television set bolted to the wall played reruns of *Here Come the Brides* all night long. He took it to be a sign from God, a sign and a prediction that he would, that he must marry this woman. But first the doctors must find out why she had the seizure and what could be done to make her well. He had done all he could, even called her mother, which had not been a pleasant task.

"What did you do to her?" Eileen Peters Stax demanded over the phone.

"I – I didn't do anything. She just collapsed." The snap in her voice made him feel small and helpless, threatened like a small rodent hiding from a cat.

"I'm on my way. You stay there, and you can explain everything when I get there." She hung up.

#

Edna didn't remember what had happened. She found herself lying on a mattress too firm for comfort, under a white sheet that gave no warmth but at least covered her embarrassment. She was alone, trapped in a body that refused to move when she told her arms to lift her hands up to her face. One foot wiggled, but her legs remained fixed.

She deduced that it must have been night, since the stark hospital lights began to darken. The lights in her room were turned off, all but a dim night light, but a white glow still entered from the hallway, since her door was open. She wondered how long a time she had been here. Time stretched out and twisted, and then she somehow left the hospital room and found herself dressed in a white satin gown, walking down the aisle to a minister standing at a podium, and a man dressed in black, his back turned to her. The minister had kind eyes, grey eyes that kept their approving gaze on her while he nodded slightly. The groom who kept his back to her turned his head slightly to get a look, and she saw Robert's face. Everything was going to be alright, she knew. She was going to marry Robert.

But where were her parents? Of course they wouldn't come. They wouldn't approve of her marriage to a working man, a man with little money and no prospects. But she loved Robert, and that was enough.

This church seemed unfamiliar and yet familiar at the same time. It was not the Episcopal church of the Blessed Sacrament, which she had attended all through her childhood. No, it must be a Protestant church of some sort. Each side wall bore three stained glass windows with scenes from the New Testament, and that was familiar, as was the podium where the minister stood. But the minister's clothing was a simple black robe, as if he were a choir member, not the lavish white satin and gold braid that she would have expected. And there was no incense, there were no candles, and the ceremony was far too simple. The minister asked each of them to take the other in sickness and health, good times and bad, forever until death, and then the best man handed Robert a simple gold band. He slipped it onto her ring finger, and then he threw back her veil and kissed her, not waiting for the minister to say that he could. In the Episcopal church, it would have been a two-ring ceremony, with Edna placing an identical gold band onto Robert's finger. Mom would not approve, but Edna was satisfied.

When Robert drove her to the City for their honeymoon at the Hotel Francis, she thought that she must be dreaming. She carefully scratched an itch on the back of her neck, where her surgical wound was still healing. This was a perfectly normal life for the two of them. And yet she felt that her hand was not real, that the chip had somehow taken over her brain, and that she had drawn Robert into her own fantasy world.

#

Edna found herself back in the hospital room with Robert sitting beside the bed, holding her hand and talking to her in low, sweet tones. She tried to say hello, but her mouth only put out bubbles of spit. Sometimes Mom was there, sitting in a chair several feet away from her bed, reading the *Chronicle*, putting a pencil to the crossword, reading aloud from every page, including the want ads. Edna knew that she meant well, but she found it annoying. Where was Robert? She wanted Robert.

She saw the raccoon shambling up to the chair where her mother sat, but she couldn't shout out a warning. Mom seemed oblivious to the presence of a furry mammal that might very likely be carrying rabies, even when it began to paw at her legs. Edna tried and tried to shout a warning, but her mouth refused to obey her brain.

Then she found herself packing up her things and moving out of her apartment, moving into Robert's little rented house near the river, a house that needed paint and nails, a new roof and new carpet. Several years went by and they had no children, although they desperately wanted little babies and toddlers running around the house. The third-graders in her classroom became little treasures, always close at hand but never in her grasp.

They saved their money and wished for a house of their own, nothing ostentatious, but at least a house with a roof that didn't leak. She put pots and pans on the floors and the furniture to catch the drips during the winter rains. She deposited almost all of every paycheck into a savings account. Still, they never seemed to have quite enough to purchase even a modest house in a suburban neighborhood. And then the magical day came. Her parents had disowned her when she married Robert, and Mom wouldn't speak to her and hung up the phone when she called, but then one day a miracle happened.

"Don't tell your mother" Dad said, standing in the doorway of her ramshackle home, and handed her a thick envelope.

She hugged him and kissed him on the cheek, and he put one gentle arm around her shoulder. She noticed that the cuff of his silk shirt was frayed, and the jacket of his silk business suit hung too loosely. Not only had he become careless about his clothing, but he had also been losing weight.

"Dad, are you eating right?" she asked.

"I'm fine," he said. "I have to go now. Tons of work to do at the office." As he turned to leave, he told her, "Remember, not a word to your mother."

"I promise." She watched her father's back walk out to his car at the curb, leaving the door open until she had seen his old Cadillac lumber down the road and out of sight. When she reached out to shut the door, she saw the envelope in her hand, forgotten in the moment of joy in having contact with her father one more time. She tore it open and found twenty bills, hundred-dollar bills, neatly stacked. No note, no writing on the envelope, just the cash. And she knew that this was her father's way of saying that he loved her. It would be enough to put a down payment on a decent house.

#

Robert struggled to bring Edna back into consciousness. Every day after work at Tower Records, he came to the hospital and sat by her side. He talked to her about everything and nothing, read aloud to her from Joyce's *Finnegan's Wake*, and sometimes played Beethoven and Mozart on a portable CD player. He searched his mind for every little thing that she had told him, the things that she loved, things that might bring her back to him. He had met the love of his life, and he couldn't bear to lose her. *Not so soon*, he almost said aloud.

Dark circles grew under his eyes from worry and lack of sleep. He lost so much weight that he had to fasten his belt one notch tighter to keep his pants up.

From time to time, he thought he saw a shadow moving about in the corners of the room. At first he put it down to the flickering of the fluorescent lights, but soon he began to suspect that something was lurking in the shadows. Perhaps a spider was stringing its web and swinging up and down, its shadow magnified by some mechanism of solid geometry. He had barely passed algebra in high school, so he never took the geometry class, since he was certain that he would have failed.

She just lay there, the IV tube feeding nutrients and drugs into her veins, a fat yellow tube leading out from the back of her head, draining the infection into a puddle on a stack of gauze next to her pillow. The doctors said that she would recover in time. He rolled that word over in his mind, *time*, as if it were a magical incantation.

The shadow jumped up onto the counter across the room and resolved into the shape of a raccoon. It seemed to be grinning at him. He looked away and then looked back, and the shadow raccoon was gone.

As he sat by her bedside, he resolved to become a success, something more than a clerk in a record store. He had music in his soul, and that music could elevate his career to something more acceptable to her family. If he were a famous composer, even if he didn't make that much money, then at least her parents might respect him. He fell asleep and dreamed of composing music, conducting an orchestra, bowing to the audience where Edna and her parents sat in the front row, beaming with pride at his artistic accomplishments.

He clearly saw his future, so much so that when he fell asleep in the chair beside her hospital bed, he dreamed of their wedding, of their little suburban house and of their beautiful daughter whose first word was not "mama" but "dada". Daddy's little angel brought light into their lives, filling the dark void of his fading love for Edna. Almost as soon as they checked out of the Hotel Francis, where they had spent their honeymoon, he found himself wanting to date other women, share his meals with other women, tell his innermost thoughts and secrets to other women.

He sent his musical compositions to publishers, to garage bands, to singers. He found an agent. He got work that paid well, but Edna's family considered his work disreputable. Advertising jingles and popular songs did little to impress their blue-blooded sensibilities.

#

Edna screamed with agony, followed by screams of joy. She had given birth to a – the doctor hesitated. "Healthy," he said. And then, "girl."

Lying in the hospital bed, she couldn't tell whether she was still in the coma that had nearly taken her life ten years ago, or whether she had found her way back to the present time, recovering from childbirth. It was all so confusing, the wrinkling and folding of time. Was she in a coma and dreaming all these years of her life, or was she thirty-two years old and dreaming of the past?

She named her daughter Angelica, the little angel who came to fill their lives with joy. Robert had grown distant, spending so much time at work ▾ his striving to get ahead. She was so proud of for composing music, for becoming successfi enough to quit his job at the record store. H parents still disapproved, since his music w themes for low-budget movies. They didr understand that even this required the ski at artist. She tried not to resent the time the the studio, but she suspected at first, ar to know, that it was not only work that took him away from her.

She asked herself whether she would have married Robert, if she had known that he would prove to be so unfaithful. She knew that, sooner or later, he would leave her for one of those other women. And yet she decided that she would marry him anyway, share his life and bear his children. Well, one child, anyway. She doted on Angelica in the hope that proving to be a worthy mother to Robert's child would keep him tied to her.

After their daughter started school, Edna became active in the community, joining social clubs and participating in charitable events. She thought about going back to her teaching job, but Robert made enough money to keep them quite well. He even bought her a mansion on the hill, thinking that it would make her happy. Didn't he know that all he needed to do was smile at her, and that would bring her joy? And yet she had to admit that she loved the gardens that surrounded the big house. They reminded her of home, her parents' home where she grown up. The gardens gave her a feeling of unity not unlike the feeling that had come over her church more than once. Time no longer mattered, miles could be torn up, appointments missed, all the sunlight on her shoulders and the shade of s, trees and grape vines in her gardens.

\#

Darkening 23

Chapter Two

Robert Wells sat in the black vinyl engineer's chair in the sound booth, leaning forward to focus on his work, sometimes scooting the chair a little on the soft sculptured carpet, which tended to catch the casters and stop their motion. With heavy liquid-filled earphones clamped around his ears, he sat listening to the track that the sound engineers had produced from what the studio musicians had played from the score, his score, for the latest low-budget horror flick *Bad Moon Rising*, another cheap tale of teenagers battling a werewolf.

The visuals flashed by on a monitor set into the console while Rob checked out the synchronization of sound track to action. In the background, softened because it was slightly out of focus, he saw a raccoon sitting up on its haunches and watching the action in the foreground. Not bad, he thought, scratching a few notes about corrections that needed to be made. The music came in too late when the werewolf grabbed its victim. The scratchy violin strokes should hit the high point a second before the visual to which it corresponded, the close-up of the monster biting its prey, not right on top of it. In any frightening scene, the slashing music must cause the viewers' hearts to race before the slasher actually touched the victim, leading the audience emotionally into the act. He knew his craft well, and he was always having to educate the technicians in the fine art of preparing the audience to be frightened out of their wits.

This movie was rather tame, compared to most of the schlock on the big screen. It was more a love story than a murder mystery, with adolescents coming to terms with their emerging sexuality, finding bonds of friendship and love. He kind of liked that.

His talent had taken him to the top in this niche of the film industry. Not bad for a high school dropout with a worthless degree in music from a second-rate correspondence school. Not bad for doing it all himself, with no help at all from his wife's wealthy family, a collection of snobs who had no use for him. It had been enough that Edna loved him, that she gave birth to their daughter, that they believed in him. Edna and Angelica inspired him, and that had been enough, once, in the hazy past.

His music blended seamlessly with the action, causing the audience to wriggle in their seats with anxious anticipation of the next bloody scene. Wells' music never sold as an album. The sappy cliché melodies and discordant fugues worked on the lowest unconscious level of the human brain and never rose to the status of a pleasant or inspiring listening experience. The critics rated it a notch below elevator music.

Sometimes Robert Wells thought that he would sell his soul to be able to write real music, not this schlock but the kind of beautiful melodies that orchestras performed in concert halls with an audience of ladies in evening gowns and gentlemen in tuxedos. Perhaps then his in-laws would finally consider him human. The only problem with that scenario was that he wouldn't earn enough money to maintain the lavish lifestyle that his high society wife demanded. And he'd probably have to give up his rented condo in town and the woman who lived there, waiting for his frequent visits.

One of the gold-vested interns came in and tried to talk to him, but Rob ignored the idiot. Didn't they know that he couldn't hear a thing with the headphones on? He saw the young man's thin lips moving, watched him push a stray lock of straight brown hair out of his eyes, then turned away to focus on his sound track. The intern, a green college student, apparently got the message and dutifully stood by until he finished his work and removed the headphones. Stuffing his notes into his day planner, Rob turned to see what he wanted.

"Your wife is on the phone. She says you're late."

"I'm always late, so far as Edna is concerned. Tell her I'll be home in twenty minutes."

Robert Wells never made it home that day. As he walked across the parking lot to his new Mercedes, heat waves rippled up from the concrete, blurring his vision. He thought that he heard footsteps behind him, but before he could turn to look, everything went black. His crumpled, nearly lifeless body was found in an alley behind the sound building on the production lot of Startling Studios and promptly carted off to the emergency room at the nearest hospital. Paramedics found his wallet on the ground, empty of money but still holding his credit cards and driver's license.

When he regained consciousness, he was lying in a hospital bed, dressed in one of those ridiculous cotton gowns that flop open in the back, revealing the patient's hinder parts. And a raccoon was sitting on the counter. It appeared to be laughing at him. A police detective interviewed him briefly, but he couldn't remember anything about the mugging. He remembered leaving the building and heading toward his car, but everything after that was a blank until he woke up in the hospital.

"This kind of amnesia is not unusual," the detective said, "but you might regain some of your memory later, when you've had time to heal. Give me a call if you remember anything at all, no matter how minor it might seem to you." He dropped one of his business cards on the bedside table and left the room.

Fortunately he hadn't suffered any internal injuries in the attack, but both of his legs and three of his ribs had hairline fractures, and he also had some serious bruises and a concussion. "Looks like someone used a blackjack on the back of his skull," the emergency room doctor had said, and he ordered an MRI (Magnetic Resonance Imaging, as Rob would learn) of his head. The sound of the machine's magnets clacking and thumping together nearly drove him crazy, even though he was wearing earplugs. He hated having his head inside that hollow white tube; it reminded him of the *Star Trek* movie where they ejected Spock's coffin into space.

The rest of his hospital stay became a blur of eating and sleeping, complaining about the slop they called food, which was an endless stream of fruit-flavored gelatin and cooked cereal with no milk or sugar, and demanding to be let out. When he didn't like the food, he would slap his thigh and the raccoon would hop up on to the side of the bed and eat it for him. He began to regard it as a pet, or maybe more than that, a friend.

When he couldn't stand the hospital bed and the hospital food any longer, he thought that he would just get up and leave, but repeated attempts to lift his head off of the pillows failed miserably. "I have work to do," he kept telling them. "I can't stay here forever."

When he slept, he suffered terrible nightmares. In one dream he was some kind of large cat watching flying lizards swoop down from the sky and hissing his defiance. In another he was a soldier in the fortress at Masada, participating in the horrible slaughter among people who chose death over Roman slavery. In yet another nightmare, he found himself among Christian heretics, living a simple life in the south of France, until the priests in their black, hooded robes came and started questioning people. He fled with others to the hilltop fortress of Montsegur, and when the French armies had them surrounded, they secretly sent three men down the treacherous back side with the treasured seed. Their own lives mattered little, so long as the seed survived.

Whenever Robert asked them when he would be released, which was every time he saw a nurse, orderly or doctor, they gave him their standard answer, "As soon as you're better." It was terribly frustrating. On the third day he persuaded his wife to bring him some real food, smuggled into his room inside her enormous purse – two cheeseburgers with fries and a chocolate shake from the local Busby Burger stand.

"No doubt this will contribute to your nightmares," she said.

"No doubt." He plunged into the burgers like a ravenous wolf.

"What was that?" Edna asked.

Robert turned his head and saw a shadow in the far corner, a shadow in the shape of a raccoon. "Oh, that's just Kelvin."

"Kelvin?"

"It's a joke. Since it's only a shadow and has no substance, then it must have a temperature of absolute zero."

"On the Kelvin scale," she said.

"Exactly."

"I thought I was the only one who saw the raccoon."

"So did I. At least we share something in common."

But that smuggled fast food was only one meal, and the daily fare of bland cardboard and mush drove him mad. When they finally did release him, the terms seemed worse than what they would have given a convict on parole. He could go home, but he would not have his freedom. They hung over his head the warning that he could end up back in the hospital, an invalid for the rest of his life, if he failed to follow doctor's orders. They also handed him the business card of a specialist in neurology, which he slid into his wallet next to the police detective's card.

After seven days in intensive care and five additional days in a private room, Rob finally found himself sitting in a wheelchair with an orderly rolling him across the parking lot to a waiting limousine, to his waiting wife. A few reporters and photographers hung around nearby, but they kept a respectful distance because Rob was only a minor celebrity, not a star. Even so, he did not like having his photograph taken when his head was all wrapped up in bandages. He wanted the public to see him always at his best.

The chauffer opened the back door of the sleek black rented limousine, revealing the stunning presence of Edna Stax Wells, her bleached blonde hair done in the latest fashion and her face painted into a seamless portrait of divine beauty. She could have graced the cover of a glossy magazine or taken the starring role in a romantic movie. Rob, having seen her in bed with all the accouterments stripped away, was impressed more by the art of deception than by her looks.

"Well," she said after the orderly helped her husband into the back seat of the limousine, a painful process of lifting, dropping and scooting over, "you certainly will go to great lengths to avoid visiting my mother."

Rob grunted, a noncommittal sound which had become his standard response whenever his wife scolded him. He tried not to listen to her when she was complaining, or really any time she said anything at all. Her alto voice with an occasional squeak, the voice which had enchanted him when they were young, grated on his ears after more than twenty years of marriage.

"Mrs. Stax sends her greetings and sympathy." The Stax family always followed the protocol of upper class society, politely but palpably reminding Robert Wells that he was only the nouveau riche and still a member of the working class, while they represented old money and fine lineage. *Lazy inheritors of their ancestors' labor*, Wells thought. He was proud of every callus on his working man's hands. He created his music as much with hands on the keyboard as with pen on paper.

He grunted again and tried to ignore his wife as the limousine gently eased across the hospital parking lot and out onto Shattuck Avenue in the business district of Berkeley, California. He loved these streets where he had grown up, a wild, fatherless boy with no money in his pocket until he got an after-school job at a record store. He used to pester the repair guys endlessly, begging them to show him how to fix broken radio sets and record players.

The radio repairs consisted mostly of testing and replacing tubes, those evacuated glass flasks of various shapes and sizes with the glowing grids inside and the metal pins, the contacts, sticking out of the bottoms. Record players, on the other hand, usually had burned our motors or worn gears.

The limousine floated down streets crowded with cars and pedestrians, all in a hurry to get somewhere and paying little attention to their surroundings. Only the panhandlers and prostitutes on the corners paid the least attention to the passing cars. College students brushed shoulders with businessmen, well-dressed ladies glared at the occasional trollop standing on the corner, and all looked both at home and out of place among the historic buildings that seemed both clean and dirty at the same time. Few if any gave the limousine a second glance. They saw them all the time and, having grown so used to their asphalt and concrete surroundings that only something extraordinary could catch their attention, they focused only on where they were going and not on where they were at this moment. They seemed as blind to the presence of a limousine carrying a minor celebrity and his beautiful wife as an owl in daylight.

Rob noticed an old derelict standing in front of the public library, holding up a cardboard sign on which he had written in crude lettering, "THE EMPIRE NEVER ENDED." The streets of the inner city were filled with all sorts of people, he told himself, including crazy people.

When Edna finally asked him about his health, Rob related what the doctor had said to him. The mugging had actually been quite serendipitous, since the MRI had discovered a growth in the occipital region of his brain, a growth that surgeons could easily remove, since it had not yet grown very large.

They had scheduled the surgery for next month, when his general health would have improved enough for his battered body to tolerate the procedure.

When they arrived at their ultra-modern steel-reinforced concrete mansion on San Antonio Avenue in the North Berkeley Hills, a male nurse and the butler helped Robert Wells up the steps to the round portico on the eastern side of the two-story structure and carried him to his upstairs bedroom in the 12,000 square foot monument. He never felt at home in this monstrosity with its white Egyptian-style columns holding up the second-floor balconies and the red-carpeted grand staircase, with gilt banisters, leading up from beside the Venetian fountain in the center of the glass-ceilinged entrance hall. Edna had selected this mansion, whereas Rob would have preferred a condominium apartment near the University. He caved in to her demands, as always, and committed himself to a $24 million mortgage that never would be paid off within his lifetime.

As soon as they laid him into his four-poster bed, he reached for the telephone.

#

"Don't worry about it," Charlie Parker told him over the phone. "Send me your notes, and I'll finish the track for *Bad Moon*."

"You'll need help. Get Harry Parch to help you."

"I said not to stress over it. You just rest up and get well."

Rob stressed over it anyway, since his reputation and six-figure income depended upon the technical brilliance of his sound tracks, works that could raise a B-movie from obscurity and bring in the millions at the box office. Dull scripts by hack writers became gripping thrillers under his expert hand. He had been blessed with an ear for suspense and a talent for evoking expectation in the audience. He still wished, often but not too fervently, that he could compose classical music of the kind that would win him respect. He hated having his in-laws look down their blue noses at him. Film producers paid him well, so well in fact that, by comparison, the hottest Broadway composer was a starving artist. He put his heart into his work, no matter how low the budget and no matter how inane the script.   Pride in workmanship might be a middle-class value, but not having been born into wealth and luxury, Rob held that value.   He hated the idea of someone else finishing his work, but his battered body kept him at home with round-the-clock nursing care. Ron Olsen took the day shift, while Mike Johnson worked through the night. His wife, knowing all too well Rob's proclivities, had vetoed the hiring of female nurses.

Rob sensed more than heard the activities of his useless brother-in-law, his sister's former husband, who occupied one of the smaller bedrooms and often made his way down to the kitchen for what he called "snacks". The man was eating more than most families, and it showed in his enormous gut. *You'd think that Timothy would have dropped in to see how I'm doing*, Rob said to himself, *but that would require some level of empathy for his fellow human beings.* He wondered why he didn't kick the bum out of his house, and why Edna didn't insist that he kick him out. Sometimes, in his more paranoid moods, he speculated that the two of them were plotting against him in some way, but he couldn't figure out a motive. Edna had the things that she wanted in life. He had purchased the mansion that she had picked out, he provided a generous allowance that financed her extravagant shopping sprees and attendance at all the gala performances and parties.

Timothy got a free ride, and all he had to do was fill in once in a while as Edna's escort when Rob's work prevented him from going out with her. Sometimes he suspected that the two of them were lovers, but Timothy didn't seem the type that Edna would go for. He was too fat, too lazy and too poor. Rob had the vague notion that Timothy earned his pocket money by doing astrology or palm reading; other than that, he seemed totally lacking in job skills. He never would have taken him in, but his sister had actually begged him to take care of her ex. That was when Sarah was dying of lymphoma, lying in a hospital bed, totally bald from the chemotherapy, looking like nothing so much as a Kewpie doll.

Every bone and muscle in his body ached, but Nurse Olsen insisted upon a daily bath followed by stretching exercises. He moaned and groaned about the exercises, and he practically screamed about the scrubbing. Soaking in a hot tub would have been soothing, but he hated the scrubbing and moving about.

"Can't you just let me lie here and soak?" Rob complained.

"You must exercise to heal properly, and we have to keep your wounds clean and change the dressings every day, or you'll get an infection."

"Yeah, well you ARE an infection. I wish you would just leave me alone."

But he suffered through the daily torture, knowing that the nurse was right and feeling thankful that Olsen let him complain as loudly as he liked, accepting his verbal abuse with a smile and never taking it personally.

Nights were easier, with Nurse Johnson dispensing his medication, tucking him in and then sitting quietly in a chair outside the bedroom door, in case he was needed. So far he had not been needed, and

Rob complained loudly about this unnecessary expense, but the doctor had insisted that he either remain in the hospital at three thousand dollars a day or obtain round-the-clock nursing care at home, which cost about three thousand dollars a week. *Home*, he mused. This two-story block of concrete, isolated from its neighbors by stone walls and manicured gardens, never did seem like home, that place where he had grown up and made friends and gone to school, gotten his first job, gone out on his first date and fallen in love.

Home was a neighborhood, not an iron-gated estate. He wished that he could escape to his apartment in town, but he went there only by himself in his own car, never with a driver and never with a nurse. *She* lived there, and nobody must ever know about *her*. *She* made life bearable, allowing him to be himself for the short time that he spent with her, accepting him as he was and approving of him. Of course, that approval came with a monetary price, but not with any emotional baggage. They knew, both of them, that they did not love each other.

After settling in for one day, Rob insisted upon getting back to work. He felt empty and useless lying in bed all the time, so in spite of the pain from three broken ribs, Rob insisted upon spending at least three hours a day at his electronic keyboard, experimenting with various combinations of tones. On the second day, he recruited Nurse Olsen and the butler to lug his keyboard and some of his other equipment into his bedroom. As usual Timothy disappeared when there was work to be done and he might be called upon to help.

"Come on," Rob insisted. "Do you want to carry me to the music room every time an inspiration hits me?"

"I want you to rest," the nurse patiently repeated.

"I thought you wanted me to exercise."

"Sitting on an organ bench is not exercise."

In the end, Rob won out by sheer persistence, more than by reason or logic. He joined Kelvin the raccoon in the music room and played his hands across the lovely keyboard.

He had won Edna's hand in marriage by the same strategy of persistence, a success which he had come to regret. He thought that he had fallen into endless, eternal love, but after the first blush of romance wore off, he found himself trapped in a loveless marriage. He had become nothing more than a prize for Edna to show off, her pet artist kept in a cage and occasionally let out on a very short leash.

He buried himself in his work to compensate for the emptiness of his home life. And then there was another woman, one who at least pretended to care for him, although he felt certain that she had at least one other lover, one who did not pay to keep her. It didn't matter, so long as she pretended to love him and made no emotional demands. She let him take a break from his hectic life once in a while. Composing music could be frenetic, especially if he didn't prepare ahead of time, before the studio contacted him with the pressing demand for another musical miracle.

He planned to have the rough draft of the score ready for the next job, the next slaughter-fest that some second or third line producer would toss his way for his magic touch. Playing with the chords, tweaking the thirds and fifths and sevenths into sad little minor key melodies and grating heart pounders, Rob laid out a possible musical scenario for a dance with the Devil or an encounter with a murderous maniac. At night he heard the music in his head, and during the day he played and recorded it on his home equipment.

By the time he got the job, he would have it already half finished, needing only to match up each musical line to a scene in the film and insert repeating phrases to match the timing to the action. That part was easy, since they were all the same, thinly plotted slasher flicks with little-known actors hoping to make it nig by getting noticed, or at least to put some food on the table with the union scale that these hack movies paid.

People seemed to think that he only grabbed opportunities that happened to come along, but he actually spent a great deal of time and effort preparing himself, getting himself ready to grab them. The parties and premieres that he detested and wished he could sleep through were opportunities to make more contacts, to get more jobs. The task of composing was almost purely mechanical, with just a touch of artistry. His touch was what made his music worth millions, and the dull social encounters were what got him the jobs that paid millions.

By the third day, he developed a migraine headache, a malady which he never had suffered before. His head throbbed while bright lights of various colors flashed inside his eyes, punctuating the pain. He saw bursts of color on the insides of his eyelids, as if tiny bombs were exploding inside his eyeballs and smashing shrapnel through his pupils into the corneas. The raccoon began jumping around the room, floating impossibly in midair and turning somersaults above Rob's head.

The nurse called in a doctor who gave him some kind of pills and advised him to lie down and rest in a darkened room. If the headache got worse, or even if it failed to improve within a day, he was to call an ambulance, since this symptom was undoubtedly caused by the brain tumor. Rob chuckled wryly at the description of this agonizing pain as a mere symptom. Surely it was a curse, a punishment for the debauched life he had been leading, a fast and frenzied life made possible partly by fame but mostly by fortune. He thought that he must have made a deal with the Devil, and this was payback.

He sometimes wished that his wife would look in on him, ask how he was doing, but aside from stopping at his bedroom door to say hello once a day, Edna stayed completely away from him during his convalescence. He began to wonder why he ever had married her, a question he had pondered often over the years, never to find the full answer. Surely, her resistance had been part of it, the fact that she represented a challenge to him.

Or perhaps a stronger motivation was that she looked so stunning on the ballroom dance floor, under the soft lights that so effectively hid her defects. Her mean mouth, concealed by the painted smile of a debutante, had fooled him and others into regarding her as a goddess of love and beauty, when in fact she represented the destroyer goddess Kali. Her custom-fitted gown, luxurious jewels and air of false nobility hid the small heart in her breast that beat fast and furious, not out of love but out of greed. She sucked the life's blood out of him to feed her own empty veins. So perhaps she was showing the quality of mercy when she ignored him, sparing the little bit of his own life force that he still possessed.

As he lay in bed with all the lights out, he began to see mathematical notations written on the walls and ceiling. They glowed like pink neon signs, numbers and symbols that he failed to understand, having flunked high school algebra; in fact, he had developed a phobia about numbers. He tried to ignore those hallucinations, but whenever he looked away from them the throbbing in his head grew worse. It was as if something wanted him to pay attention to a message of great importance. The glowing pink numbers and other symbols appeared on the walls and ceiling as if scratched into the surface by claws, then erased by the swipe of a furry paw and replaced with other numbers and symbols, always glowing like pink neon lights. Gradually he began to recognize frequencies, numbers that stood for musical tones.

He knew from his musical education that each note was a vibration that could be measured mathematically, but he hadn't given it much thought, preferring to compose his music by intuition. He possessed a feel for the music, so why bother with the difficult and frustrating mathematics of tones and scales?

The more he studied the numbers on the walls, the less his head throbbed. Still, he did not understand what was so important about them. Finally, as if frustrated, whatever entity had been writing on the walls suddenly scratched a series of parallel lines into the wall with steel claws, then laid out musical notation, the twisted letter S of the treble clef and the backwards letter C of the bass clef, with round whole notes, flagged half and quarter notes, eighth notes and even a few squiggly little grace notes.

Rob sat up straight in his bed and stared at the composition that lay before his eyes. Studying it carefully, he played it in his head, hummed it to himself and memorized every detail, spending what seemed like forever in reverie, hearing the music laid out before him and savoring each delicious tone. At length he got up and ran to his keyboard to play and record the music. He barely noticed the pain in his ribs and the rubbery feeling in his knees from his partially healed injuries. Nurse Johnson hurried into the room, asking what was wrong, but Rob waved him off and placed his hands lovingly on the keyboard.

He sat there in the dim glow of the nightlight, caressing the keyboard and preparing a melodic line to be recorded on CD. On the wall facing him, a rectangle appeared. Then a line crossed through it diagonally, forming the hypotenuse of a right triangle, all of the lines glowing, the rectangle in pink and the hypotenuse in green. Rob stared at it while he picked out the melody on his keyboard, his fingers knowing all of the keys by touch, his eyes needing no light to see them. The green hypotenuse rotated, its far end coming up until it was parallel with the top of the rectangle, and then a new rectangle formed with that green line as its long side.

A voice in his head, the familiar voice of his high school math teacher Dr. Bell, said, "This is the Golden Rectangle, the Golden Mean." He regarded the new rectangle as a thing of beauty, and he felt relieved that it didn't require any numbers to calculate and draw it. The voice spoke again, saying, "The most beautiful music has the shape of the Golden Rectangle."

This music was no sound track, no hack piece for a substandard horror film. This was the heavenly music of the spheres, a classical symphony sprinkled with a rock-and-roll back beat and just a touch of jazz-blues. It rose and fell like Beethoven's *Eroica*, turned playful like a Mozart aria, then grew somber like the "Moonlight" sonata.

He spent the next few days of his convalescence studying the writing on the wall and composing masterpieces of avant-garde music. Driven like Beethoven striving to beat the deadline of his growing deafness, Robert Wells turned out sheets of musical notation and recordings of his feeble attempts to play it on a keyboard with no orchestra to back him up, reveling in the beauty of this gift from whatever muse had deigned to bestow it upon him. He thought that he might have sold his soul to the Devil in exchange for this music. This was the stuff of genius, the artistry that he never had hoped to achieve and therefore never had attempted. He began to fear that this new inspiration was coming from his brain tumor and that he would lose it all after the surgery. He grew increasingly apprehensive as the scheduled day approached.

"It's okay, Dad," his daughter said.

He looked up from his keyboard to ask her how she had managed to enter his room without him noticing, but he saw nobody. *I'm going nuts*, he told himself. *Hearing voices is not normal. Must be symptoms caused by the tumor.*

As the days passed, and his music developed, he increasingly feared the surgery and the loss of his new talent, his genius, more than losing his mind or even dying.

#

Chapter Three

Edna Stax Wells avoided her husband, preferring to enjoy the company of her bridge club and the festive atmosphere of the shopping malls rather than spend dreary hours in a darkened room with a man who groaned almost every time he moved and complained loudly whenever the nurse made him do the exercises that the doctor had prescribed. She looked in on him every day, hoping to find him cheerful and wanting her company, but he practically chased her out with his grumpy attitude.

He complained about everything, from the food to the color of his carpet. He complained the most loudly about his daily exercises. She protested that it couldn't hurt him that much to stretch, or else people wouldn't do it every time they woke up in the morning. Besides, she didn't want to upset him while he was healing from his injuries. Lately they had been arguing over everything and nothing, so she thought it best to leave him alone and let him rest. Even when Rob's headaches went away, Edna stayed away, now that he had that contemptible keyboard right beside his bed. She never had liked his music, considering it a necessary banality in their otherwise respectable life. *Let him wallow in his misery,* she thought, *and let him plunk out his movie noises, but I have better things to do.*

She took long walks in the garden, reminding herself never to look at a clock or a watch. Time must not rule her life, at least not the way it had ruled her mother's life. She loved watching the monarchs and painted ladies hanging around the butterfly bush, a fat shrub with tiny purple flowers. She looked in wonder at the century plant, which had just bloomed; its central spike had grown like an engorged penis, yes, that was what it looked like, the male organ of a green plant, and little white flowers had popped out all over that spike. Her feet crunched the gravel on the garden path, reminding her of how it felt to be grounded, literally, in the soil that nurtured life. There, off to the left, she was a little furry creature peeking out from between the hedges. The black mask across a gray face told her that it was the resident raccoon, Kelvin. He popped out onto the path and skittered away, so she followed him.

Kelvin disappeared around the corner, behind the patch of canna lilies. She followed, not expecting to catch up with the little varmint. When she came around the curve in the gravel path, she confronted a sight that she had never seen before, in the middle of her garden, a thing that could not exist. The entrance to a cave opened before her, a rock cavern that never had been there before.

Curiosity, perplexity and a modicum of fear alternated in her consciousness while she shifted her weight from one foot to the other, then back again, contemplating whether to enter the rock cavern. Curiosity won out, and she stepped inside.

#

Rob felt utterly miserable, except when he was composing his new music. He didn't care what kind of entity was feeding it to him, or even whether it was his own mind sinking into insanity. It was mad, in a way, to give up his lucrative movie music for the kind of artistic compositions that paid so much less. He worried about how he was going to pay the bills for his mansion, his new Mercedes and his mistress, but every time he tried to work on the movie theme, the migraine struck him and laid him out again. The one bright spot for Rob alighted when his daughter Angelica came home from college for a few days to spend time with poor debilitated Dad.

This perky dark-haired beauty, an honor student at UC Davis who was studying to be a veterinarian, almost made his loveless marriage worthwhile. Here was a soul that resonated with his, and he felt certain that they had been lovers in a previous life. If he ever ended up in Hell, surely Angelica would reach down from Heaven and pull him out. She might even be called upon to banish that pesky raccoon. It had begun peeing on the carpet, and the nasty odor of stale urine assaulted his nose.

They exchanged a few pleasantries, and he drank in her image as she sat in the bedside chair, telling him all about her classes and her internship with a horse doctor and anything at all. It was a joy just to look at her, and he thought that she had the voice of an angel.

"Did you hear about the UFO?" she asked.

"No."

"Well, it was the strangest coincidence, I mean it happened less than a block from where you were working on that day, you know."

Rob nodded. Yes, he knew what day, the day when somebody mugged him as he walked out to his car. He had always wondered how they managed to get past the security guards. It wasn't as if just anybody could wander in through the gates. The guards were supposed to stop every car and look at identification before lifting the arm that stopped them at the gate. A twelve-foot concrete block wall kept out people who might try to sneak in on foot. Yet the mugger had managed to get in and out unnoticed, as invisibly as a black cat in the dark, and as silently as if on the wings of an owl.

"Well, anyway, it turns out that it was an advertising balloon that got loose from its tethers and lost its buoyancy. It came down and scared a bunch of people who thought they saw a flying saucer. Isn't that funny? Maybe they should make a movie about it."

Rob smiled and almost laughed, but laughing would have hurt his ribs. He adored his daughter, and everything she said or did pleased him. The fact was, he would have divorced Edna years ago, if he thought it wouldn't upset Angelica. But he knew that she would be deeply hurt if her parents split up, so he endured the constant nagging, punctuated by periods of silence and even absence that his wife inflicted upon him for no other reason than that he lacked the polished manners of a blue-blooded member of the social elite. He tried at first, when they were young, but he never could remember which fork to use for his salad, or what to say when introduced to some distant cousin, or how to behave in the smoky drawing rooms of the clubs he had been forced to join, organizations filled with stuffy old men who sat around telling dirty jokes and then had the nerve to call him gauche because his necktie said, "I Love You, Dad". His daughter had given him that tie, so he wore it proudly, no matter what they thought of it.

He begged Angelica to come with him to the ribbon-cutting ceremony at Horror Haven, the new theme park dedicated to all things macabre and grisly, and she relented, midterm exams notwithstanding. Edna came along, too, encouraged by the prospect of seeing her own face on the evening news. For Rob it would be his last public act before the dreaded brain surgery, an ordeal that at best would leave him an invalid for several weeks and at worst, well, he didn't want to think about that. He tried to focus on the fact that Horror Haven was using some of his best movie sound tracks to back up the computer-generated virtual reality sequences which they had devised to entertain visitors to the park.

As the day of the ribbon cutting approached, he tried to work on his next sound track. Sitting at the keyboard, he plunked out the staccato lead-in to a smashing event, such as shattering glass. As his fingers pressed the keys, his migraine came back with such fury that he had to lie down again. It seemed as if his muse were patiently but firmly teaching him to make beautiful music, not the commercial schlock that paid his mortgage and his daughter's tuition. He wondered whether it was a guardian angel, or the Devil himself, who was forcing him to give up his livelihood.

#

Edna sat in the cave, where she found the floor as soft as her couch cushions, and watched a display of multicolored lights playing across the walls and ceiling. Somewhere in the depths of the cave, a voice rumbled, whispering words that she couldn't quite make out. Then she woke up, wondering how she had gotten into bed, fallen asleep and experienced such a magical dream, when only moments before, she had been walking in her garden and following a raccoon.

Rob was forced to attend the ribbon-cutting event in a motorized wheelchair that he hadn't quite gotten the hang of, and with Nurse Olsen in tow, since his injuries had not completely healed and the brain tumor might cause some trouble. He felt stiff in the black tuxedo that the butler and nurse had stuffed him into, the cummerbund hiding the corset which supported his healing ribcage, the clip-on bow tie allowing some neck room for him to breathe and speak. If they had fastened the top button and knotted a real tie around his collar, he would have been twice as miserable. If it were up to him, he would attend the gala in blue jeans and a T-shirt, but he made this great sacrifice for Edna's sake and for the media photographers. Truth be told, he did like to look his best out in public. The owner of the park, Herbert Craft, shone like a sapphire in his blue sequined jacket as he handed the scissors to Rob. Herb looked immaculate with his black hair slicked back and his tailored suit gleaming in the sunlight. Rob felt at home with this high-powered public relations man, much more so than with the stuffed business suits inhabiting the clubs where Edna's family had insisted upon sponsoring and purchasing Rob's membership. Edna glittered with shimmering makeup, a full length gown and a diamond necklace.

Angelica, dressed in a plain but tasteful peach-colored slacks suit, beamed with pride in her father. Other important people stood around while photographers snapped and flashed their photographs. Rob held the scissors on the edge of the cherry-red ribbon that stretched across the park entrance, dutifully posing for the photographers for a few minutes before the actual slicing of the ribbon. At a table just inside the park, waiters patiently stood by with champagne bottles ready to be uncorked. Rob tired of smiling, of holding up his heavy arm, and at last he decided that it was time to cut the ribbon. As the blades bore down, more cameras snapped and flashed.

At last he rolled into the park, surrounded by reporters and important people, to the sound of popping corks and polite applause. With all that pomp and ceremony, you would have thought that it was the opening of opera season, rather than of a venue designed to provide cheap thrills and chills to tourists in T-shirts.

He couldn't be sure when everything went black, but it seemed like a replay of the mugging. He awoke in a strange place filled with darkness and the screams of people in agony.

#

The alien slugs on board the flying saucer, which was not an advertising balloon after all, observed their subject with interest. They had their space ship buried under the ground in a small local park now, so the inhabitants of this planet could neither see it nor touch it while they conducted their research. The subject seemed able enough to learn, if not exactly willing, to produce a lovely harmony with depth and meaning. They had tried at first to communicate in the universal language of mathematics, but apparently it was not universal, after all.

This subject seemed to lack even the most basic understanding of numbers, so they reached out through his one undeniable talent, and that was music. They had been hoping to produce through him a unified field theory, but they would have to settle for a symphony. The organic implant they had inserted into his brain had a limited period of usefulness, since the batteries would soon wear out, and they hoped to have the subject completely trained before that happened. The limit was probably less than two months, and they had already wasted more than five weeks trying to teach him the fundamentals of musical composition. They had newly hatched slugs who could learn faster and do better. The dominant species on this planet was obviously quite backward.

It should be noted here that all slugs, including alien slugs, are stone deaf. They simply have no ears. However, they are capable of feeling the tonal vibrations and calculating the most pleasing frequencies. Using their advanced mathematics, they developed harmonies of tactile sensation that pleased them as they slid around the inner hull of their craft on trails of mucous. Slugs do have acceptable eyesight, along with a refined olfactory sense, and alien slugs are extremely intelligent.

When they saw the theme park, they grew curious about what was inside the building, a hexagon of white stucco with a door leading into each of its six sides. Now, the fact is that alien slugs possess insatiable appetites and nearly insatiable curiosity. Sliding around on their mucous trails inside their flying saucer, they communicated with each other by touching tentacles. Within a few minutes, they had all agreed that they must get the subject to open one of those doors and look inside the building.

Unfortunately, they lost control when he entered the white room. They soon determined that the theme park's computer had taken over communications with the implant. The alien slugs considered blasting that computer into its component atoms, but this new scenario intrigued them. They wanted to see how it would play out and how much they could influence the events. Reaching their electronic tendrils into the park's computer, they produced the alien slug equivalent of popcorn and settled down to enjoy the show, taking turns tweaking the details of the performance at the keyboard of their ship's computer console.

#

Startled by his new and disturbing surroundings, Rob Wells stood up and suddenly realized that all of the pain of his broken bones and bruised muscles had gone away. In fact, he felt better than he had in years. Looking around as his eyes grew accustomed to the darkness, he found himself in an underground cavern, standing on the edge of a precipice that fell deep into the Earth, a nearly bottomless pit filled with orange flames and screaming people. The only light in this dark pit flickered from those flames, assaulting his eyes like a strobe, repeatedly blinding him with light and heat, then leaving him in blackness, alternating almost faster than his pupils could adjust. The sound of their screams told him that the vague forms deep below were people, even though he couldn't make out their exact shapes. The scene seemed familiar, like something out of a book that some English teacher had once forced him to read. He backed away from the edge and walked sideways around the cavern, keeping his back against the wall as he moved, seeking an opening where he might escape from this horrible place. As he circled the room, he began to forget his name, his past and nearly everything about his life before this moment. A strange, sad melody played inside his head, as if his life now had a sound track.

He nearly shrieked when he saw an invisible hand drawing glowing orange numbers on the opposite wall of the cavern. It was not so much that it startled him as that he saw the dreaded quadratic equations, which he never had been able to solve! In an instant he found himself sitting in math class at Berkeley High, chewing on his yellow number two pencil and struggling with all those Xs and Ys, doubled and squared. Sweat broke out on his forehead. He must have been daydreaming in the middle of the algebra exam, and now he found himself completely stumped by the problem. Then a voice entered into his mind, a familiar feminine voice that patiently explained it to him.

"You solve the equation," she said, "by multiplying each number inside the first set of parentheses by each number inside the second set of parentheses."

He still did not quite understand, so she walked him through it, one step at a time. "X times X is X squared, and don't worry about what X is. It doesn't matter. X times Y is XY, and don't worry about what that is, either."

The soothing tones of her voice settled his jangled nerves, and it did begin to make sense to him. He carefully wrote down each step with his number two pencil, and soon he had the problem solved. The solution was X squared plus Y squared plus two XY. Perhaps he would not flunk algebra, after all.

Still unsure of who he was or how he got here, the teenage boy walked home from school, even though he did not know the way. He was young, flexible and able to bounce back from the shock of his situation, absorb it and deal with it. The feminine voice guided him down the streets of Berkeley, ignoring the prostitutes and panhandlers leaning on the lamp poles and haunting the corners, and he soon came to a weather-beaten house made of white clapboard with an asphalt shingle roof. His feet seemed familiar with the two steps up to the covered porch and two strides to the front door. Turning the brass knob and pulling open the door, he called out, "Mom, I'm home!"

A rustling sound from upstairs told him that his mother was in bed, probably reading another one of her Reader's Digest condensed classics. She made it a habit to read a book every day, every two days at the most. He went to the kitchen and opened the refrigerator, changed his mind and closed it. His body seemed to know every inch of this house, even though his mind found it unfamiliar. The hardwood floors and braided rugs were clean, almost too clean. The kitchen counters were uncluttered and the bathroom was sparkling. He soon learned that his mother never did the cleaning. It was all his own work that kept the house in order, and he needed order in his life. He obsessed about any little thing that got out of place, whether it was a stray spoon on the kitchen counter or a dust bunny under the sofa.

The next day at school, during nutrition break, two boys called out to him. He didn't realize at first that they were talking to him, since he didn't remember his own name. He didn't remember their names, either, at first.

"That algebra test was the pits," Bobby said. The dark-haired boy playfully punched him on the arm.

"Yeah, I think I might have flunked it," Bruce said. "How did you do?" The boy with the military-style crew cut looked at him expectantly.

"I think I might have passed," he said noncommittally.

The boy learned from his friends that his name was Teddy and that his summer job application had been accepted. He was about to go to work sweeping floors at the local record store. His heart filled with joy that he would have somewhere to go on the hot summer afternoons, a place where he could listen to the latest pop tunes, lounge in the rare luxury of air conditioning and even get paid for it. He might even meet girls, something of which his mother strongly disapproved. But first he had to pass his final exams, and since this was his senior year, he must pass them or spend the entire summer in school, making up the credits needed for graduation. He had already decided to take the job, even if it meant never finishing high school, never getting a diploma. Mom would throw a fit, but she would get over it. She must be accustomed to her son disappointing her by now; she always said so. Teddy was just beginning to understand the world in which he found himself. The process of anamnesis, of unforgetting, was just beginning to work in his mind.

#

The alien slugs watched the subject frantically trying to escape the Inferno, a feeble amusement park imitation of Hell, and they disapproved of this misuse of such an advanced computer for cheap thrills. Entering deep into its circuitry, they made some adjustments to the software, enabling the entire amusement park to act as a teaching machine. Their subject would be rewarded for good decisions and punished for bad ones. They hoped that he would learn the lesson before the implant's batteries, which were designed to last six or seven weeks, went dead. In fact, they even considered an intervention to replace the batteries, if the need arose. They accelerated the program to run weeks and months through their subject's mind in a matter of minutes, fearing that the other inferior creatures might take him out of the room before they had completed their study. One thing puzzled them: the voice of the girl did not seem to be coming from the amusement park computer, and the alien slugs certainly were not the source of it, either. They diligently searched for information on this phenomenon, but the subject had severely limited data; he didn't seem to know much about it.

They studied the memory banks of the computer, searching for some explanation of that feminine voice. The closest thing to it was something called Sybil, a mythical being that lived inside a leather flask hung on the wall of a cave in ancient Greece.

She foretold the future for great and noble warriors and kings. The computer held data about a variety of myths and legends, but that information was only superficial, having been stored for the frivolous purpose of entertaining tourists. The alien slugs slid around on the interior walls of their space ship in utter frustration at the lack of meaningful information. They wished that they could access the computer at the local library, but they didn't seem to be able to get their subject to go there. He was stuck in the white room, unconscious in his wheelchair, living a fantasy that came from three sources: the amusement park's computer, the alien slugs and his own mind. These highly intelligent alien slugs couldn't understand the meaning of the feminine voice because they knew nothing of the power of love or of family feelings. Once they laid their eggs, their offspring were on their own.

After digging deep into Robert Wells' brain, they decided to grant him his greatest wish, that he could start his life over and live it again. He seemed to think that he would make better decisions, if he had it all to do over again. His memories indicated that his troubles all began in his senior year in high school, so they started him off at age seventeen.

#

Teddy's first real kiss with a real girl happened in a listening booth at Magic Music, where his boss Martin Munt had asked him to fill in at the cash register when one of the regular clerks called in sick. Putting aside the broom, he had turned to the task of selling 45 RPM singles and 33 1/3 long-playing albums, LPs. He loved to carry the vinyl disks by their edges, so as not to get fingerprints on the grooves, and set them gently onto the turntable. Not too long ago, records had been fragile clay tablets coated with shellac, a glue-like substance made from the chitin exoskeletons of millions of beetles. Science had developed vinyl as part of the war effort, in an attempt to find a substitute for rubber, and now it had hundreds of civilian uses that enriched their lives.

Candy seemed more interested in him than in Perry Como, and so he asked her out. Always a shy boy, he suffered terribly from raging hormones that had no outlet. He walked down the aisles making certain that every record album was in its proper place in the wooden racks, every stack of singles arranged in alphabetical order by artist and title. When Candy invited him into the listening booth, claiming that she didn't know how to work the record player, he followed her without question. When he worked up the courage to ask her out, she said maybe, and then she smiled and said yes.

On the walk home, he felt so happy that he actually stopped to drop a nickel into a panhandlers cup. He smiled and waved at the hookers but kept on walking. The sun had already gone down, but the streetlights hadn't come on yet, so only the afterglow of twilight lit the streets and sidewalks. Near the front door of the post office, he saw a derelict holding up a cardboard sign with crude hand-drawn lettering that read, "THE END IS COMING, THINGS ARE NOT AS THEY APPEAR". He saw something familiar about the ragged man with a tall, thin frame and scraggly yellow hair, but he couldn't place him, so he kept on walking. If the derelict recognized Teddy, he gave no sign of it. But as Teddy kept on walking, the old man with the cardboard sign began to follow him, until they came to a drug store. Teddy paced back and forth in front of the window-glass door, thinking of buying some condoms, but he felt too embarrassed to go inside. He was just beginning to walk away, when three young punks approached and began harassing the street-corner prophet. They pulled at his coat, laughing and hurling insults, acting like stupid fools. Teddy turned to watch, in case it got serious. It did. One of the punks knocked the man down and began kicking him.

"Hey, stop that!" Teddy shouted, but they ignored him and began taking turns kicking the old man in the ribs.

Teddy knew that he couldn't take on the three of them by himself, and there wasn't anybody else around, so he looked for a pay phone. Luckily, the drug store had one just inside the door. He went inside and picked up the receiver and, fishing in his pockets for a dime, he realized that he had no idea what the number was for the police department. He thought of dialing the Operator "O", but he didn't think he could tell her exactly where he was, or which police department to contact. "What's the address here?" he called out, but the pharmacist must have been in the back room, since nobody answered him.

Then he remembered that he had a card in his wallet, the card from the police detective. Pulling out his leather wallet from his back pocket, he found that it contained only a couple dollar bills and his California driver's license. Staring at it, he wondered why he thought that he had a police detective's business card. He didn't know any cops, so what was that about?

He was about to go ahead and dial the Operator "O", when he heard one of the punks shout, "He's calling the heat!" Then they ran away.

Teddy went back outside to help the derelict get up, but he had disappeared. He was sure that the old man couldn't have gone anywhere without him seeing, but he definitely was not there, not any more than a police detective's business card was in his wallet. Since he couldn't do anything about it, he shrugged and walked the rest of the way home, letting the incident fall out of his mind.

#

In the darkness of the movie theatre he held hands with the girl who had actually opened her mouth to kiss him, and he felt electricity flowing through his body. He started to reach inside her blouse, but she slapped his hand. Somewhere in the distance, he thought that he heard a blood-curdling scream. The picture on the movie screen, which he had hardly noticed, showed orange flames licking at naked bodies. Teddy folded both of his hands in his lap, and the picture changed back to a John Wayne cowboy movie. He thought that it was *Red River*, but it might have been *She Wore a Yellow Ribbon*. In the presence of Candy, with her warm body and soft perfumed hair, all of the John Wayne cowboy movies blended into one story in his mind. He never could remember which one was which, especially not when he was holding hands with her. He dated her all summer and into the fall.

Candy looked familiar, a curvy figure topped with golden hair and sparkling eyes of an indeterminate color, and her voice sounded a little bit like the one that had helped him with quadratic equations, enabling him to pass high school algebra and graduate on time, so he could accept his job at the record store without getting a big lecture from his mother about the importance of an education. He knew that there was something familiar about both voices, the one in his head and the one in Candy's throat, but he couldn't place them. All he knew for certain was that he had to marry this girl.

As he walked her home, they chatted about their families, their classmates and other things that seemed vitally important to their young lives. Teddy barely noticed the uneven spots where tree roots had lifted up one or another square of the sidewalk, he forgot to avoid stepping on the cracks, and he almost tripped a couple times, he was so absorbed in his new girlfriend.

"Bobby got sent to Korea," Teddy said, starting up a conversation just to hear her voice.

"Why aren't you in the Army?" Candy asked. "You'd look handsome in a uniform."

"They wouldn't take me."

"Why? Is there something wrong with you? Flat feet?"

"High blood pressure." He was painfully aware, as his mother had told him so many times, that the most common reason for the Army to reject a recruit was homosexuality, and he was beginning to feel anxious about his own orientation, even though he still adored girls and couldn't imagine being with a man. Perhaps it was the atmosphere in his best friend Larry's house, where the two boarders were also rather effeminate. He planned to take a room there, himself, over the strenuous objections of his mother. He decided that he must find some other place to stay, some place other than Mom's house. He was all grown up now, but she still tried to boss him around. She set his curfew, criticized his clothing and even ordered him to comb his hair before leaving the house.

Larry's boarding house seemed the perfect place for him, but he felt uneasy about the sexual orientation of the residents there. Once he settled in there, he would find it difficult to move out, since he would miss the intelligent conversation from these artists, two poets and a classical musician. He already enjoyed their nights out in The City, San Francisco, at the Purple Onion, a homosexual bar where he dared not set foot without a companion. He also enjoyed not having to travel on foot or by bus, having no car of his own; he felt eternally grateful for the benefit of riding around in Larry's Plymouth sedan. His mother protested with venom when he told her that he was moving out of her house, predicting that he was heading toward his doom, but she did let him take the big Magnavox radio with the booming bass response.

"That thing always drives me crazy," she told him. "It's like hearing disembodied spirits when that thing is on." She loved live stage performances and the movies, but she had an intense aversion to radio broadcasts. It was probably the fact that you couldn't see the performers over a radio. Her sister, who died young, had delved deeply into spiritualism. Teddy figured that his mother found the disembodied voices over the radio too much like the spirit voices coming through a trance medium.

"Maybe if you went to the doctor," Candy said, "he could give you some pills, and then the Army would take you."

Teddy was about to argue about the reasons why they should not go to war, when they reached Candy's front door.

"I'd ask you in," she said, "but Mama is sick, so I don't think it's a good idea." She kissed her hand and blew the kiss in his direction, then disappeared behind the door, which clacked shut with more force than seemed necessary.

Teddy suspected that Candy would not go out with him again, since he did not have a uniform and was not going to Korea. He walked home with an ache in his heart, determined to try again, to ask her not only to go out with him, but to marry him and be his wife. It was partly that she was the first girl that he ever kissed, and partly that she presented a challenge. The more she rejected him, the harder he strove to convince her to be with him. He had a good job, and he wasn't going to die in the rice paddies of Asia, so she ought to see that marrying him would be in her best interests. Part of him said that this plan was futile, that Candy wanted a soldier and not a boy who wasn't good enough to go off to the killing fields, but even so, he had little competition with most of the other young men off to war. If he persisted, he knew that he could win her heart.

He studied the newsreels that the movie theatre played before the main feature, especially when they showed one of the President's speeches. Teddy hoped that Truman would not get re-elected; the peace-time draft that he instituted even before they went into Korea had decimated his graduating class. The supposedly democratic south under President Syngman Rhee was no more than a puppet of the Allies who had agreed to divide Korea after World War Two. The north under dictator Kim Il-Sung was no better, being a satellite of the Soviet Union. Teddy believed, along with millions of other patriotic Americans, that they should stay out of this foreign war and let the Koreans determine their own destiny.

When he got home, his roommates were fiddling with a big steel machine on the kitchen counter.

"They got an espresso maker," Larry explained.

"It's going to save us a ton of money," George said. "It'll be tons cheaper than the coffee houses."

"Yeah, if we can ever get it to work," Michael complained.

"It was a steal at Pier One," George said.

"And now we know why," Larry said.

Teddy examined the machine, which looked like a restaurant percolator, a fat steel cylinder with a steel tube sticking out on the left side and a steel handle on the right, squatting on the kitchen counter. It reminded him of something from a robot monster movie with one red light and one yellow light on its face looking like mismatched eyes, the on/off toggle switch for a nose and its mouth on the underside where the little tray of coffee grounds fitted into the slot. The base had an open area under the mouth, where the cup would sit to receive the espresso. "Is it plugged in?" he asked.

"Yes!" the other three said in unison.

"Well, what's the handle for? Have you tried pulling it?"

They hadn't. George pulled the handle, and thick brown liquid poured out into the coffee cup. It took them another week to figure out that the tube on the left was for frothing milk to make latte.

In the evenings after work, they enjoyed sitting around listening to the Magnavox and sipping espresso, while Teddy listened to their discussions of literature. He hadn't read much, himself, so he couldn't contribute much to the conversation.

Friday afternoon after work, he skipped the espresso and knocked on Candy's door to ask her to go out dancing. To his surprise, she said yes. He felt elated and miserable at the same time, as if he were running headlong to his own doom.

He began to hear music in his head, the soundtrack of his life, an ominous bass beat like the approach of a killer shark.

#

Chapter Four

Not one of the dozens of people at the grand opening of Horror Haven had seen the man in the wheelchair leave the group, and not one of them had any idea which of the half dozen attractions he had entered. All they knew was that Robert Wells had gone missing, and they must find him. No doubt his brain tumor had caused him to behave erratically. What a shame that the doctors had sent him home, instead of keeping him confined in the hospital where he would be safe. The park owner, Herbert Craft, led Wells' wife and daughter into the heart of the complex, the control center where the mainframe computer was located, and where they could use the park's many security cameras to search for their husband and father.

The attractions were bare white rooms, and since none of the events had been started yet, there was nothing of interest in them, nothing to prevent them from seeing Robert Wells if he had entered one of those rooms. Everything that happened in this park consisted of computer generated holograms, scenes of horror designed to frighten visitors without any danger of physical harm. The walls and floors were covered with soft foam to prevent any accidental injuries if they panicked and tried to run away. Surely Rob Wells had gone into one of those rooms, and so he would be safe from harm and easy to find.

"What the –" Craft stuttered. "That is not one of our attractions."

The security monitor showed a dark cavern with a fiery pit in the center, and a teenage boy walking in circles around the edge of the pit with his back pressed to the wall.

"Who is that?" Edna Stax Wells asked.

"No idea. This is not in the computer program. Unless something has gone haywire. It looks like Dante's Inferno, but who is that boy? He isn't part of it."

"It's Dad," Angelica said. It looks just like his picture in his high school yearbook." She wondered why her mother had failed to recognize him.

Craft picked up a microphone and flipped the communication switch for the room where that scene was playing out. "Mr. Wells," he said. "Listen to me, Mr. Wells."

The boy on the screen paid no attention, seeming not to hear the voice on the intercom.

"Let me talk to him," Angelica said, grabbing the microphone. "Dad, it's me. Listen to me."

"You keep talking," Craft said, "and I'll go in there and bring him out."

Unfortunately, he found the door locked. Since he was unable to open it, he would have to call someone in to break down the door.

#

Mom had warned him about the evils of that rhythm and blues, with its jungle beat and obscene lyrics, but Teddy just couldn't help listening to its intriguing harmonies. She was even more adamant about rock and roll, with the back beat borrowed from the best of jazz-blues, but he began listening to that new form, too, because he found it fascinating. Besides, even Pat Boone, one of Mom's favorite singers, was recording tunes like "Tutti Fruity" and "Ain't That a Shame". Mom also disapproved of his dating girls. Fortunately, his small salary at the record store was just enough to enable him to rent a room in a house where his best friend from high school also lived. Larry was a weird kid, even stranger than Teddy, a poet who never seemed to have a date, who went to the senior prom stag, who seemed to spend all his time reading and writing. He worked at a local bookstore that sold new and used comics and magazines with florid covers. Larry introduced Teddy to fantasy fiction, the trashy reading material that Mom never allowed in her house; she insisted that only good quality literature enter through her door, in the form of Reader's Digest condensed books. After several months, Larry also let him in on the biggest secret of his life: that he never dated because he did not go for girls. So that explained why Mom was always shrieking at Teddy that he would end up "queer" if he moved out of her house! But it did not explain why she objected so strenuously when he dated girls. Teddy felt pulled in all directions whenever Mom was around, so he tried to avoid her. Somehow, however, his feet seemed to carry him over to her house for a visit every Saturday afternoon.

"I'm going to ask Candy to marry me," he said while stirring a spoon of sugar into his coffee.

"You're too young," Mom protested. "And that girl is no good for you. She's just plain no good. You'll end up in prison or dead or worse."

Teddy knew what "worse" meant: homosexual. He had given up arguing with his mother about whether it was a sin or a crime, and tried not to bring up the subject or to say anything about his best friend Larry who, in her opinion, was headed straight to Hell. Teddy admired Larry's poetry, which had won him awards and even a little money. His friend wrote about little animals in their fur pelts, sunning themselves on flat branches or in grassy meadows, keeping a watchful eye on the sky for predatory birds while scrabbling through the brush for edible grasses and seeds. Larry must possess a gentle soul, to write with such tenderness about squirrels and rabbits with such passion.

"Look at me when I'm talking to you," Mother said. "Listen to me, and don't let your mind wander off like always. Candy will lead you into perdition." Her dragon's voice emanated from the sweetest little old lady face, powdered and made up, framed by short curls of silvery gray hair. The incongruity of her voice with her appearance bothered Teddy.

"She's a nice girl," he said. "She's enrolled at the university, and she's living with her parents."

"Why would anybody want to get married when they just got out of high school? You don't know what you're getting into, and it won't last. She will ruin you."

Teddy left his mother's house in a daze, wondering how they had gotten into yet another argument, one of hundreds that always ended with her informing him that he was a terrible son who did not respect his mother and who was heading for perdition and refusing to listen to reason. He wandered aimlessly along the narrow residential streets until he found himself walking past a small shop that sold liquor and groceries at highly inflated prices, heading toward the Lucky Dog Pet Shop. He had no idea why he had come this way, since he had no pets and no plans to get a pet. On the next corner the same derelict, the one he had seen last week, stood holding a cardboard sign with hand-drawn letters that read, "YOU ARE ON THE WRONG PATH, TURN BACK TO THE LIGHT". He smiled, amused at the nonsensical messages offered by the obviously mentally disturbed old man. Teddy kept walking until he reached a little city park with dirt paths winding between tall elm trees. The sun was going down behind the trees, and that made him think of the hundred acre wood in *Winnie the Pooh*, even though this park was hardly more than half an acre. As darkness closed in around him, a great weight of melancholy pressed down on his chest. He fell to his knees and sobbed, wishing that he had not told his mother about his plan to marry his sweetheart, wishing that he had not come to see his mother at all. He should have stayed in his room in Larry's big house with three sofas in the living room, a spacious kitchen and four bedrooms and two bathrooms upstairs, where he had a view of the city streets from his window. His time would have been better spent sitting up in bed and reading fantasy fiction.

The alien slugs were beginning to suspect that the subject had feelings for other people, that they might be more than servants or accessories. And here he was, after all those thoughts about making different decisions in his life, deciding to marry the same girl again, just like the first time around. They decided to use his emotions to guide him onto a more productive path. They set up another scenario to both punish and instruct him on how the course of this simulated life should proceed. They reached into the computer's memory for a scenario near the entrance to Hell, but not in the pit of fire. It should be a scene in a dark wooded area, where the subject would experience fright but not real harm.

When he got back up on his feet, Teddy thought that he would quickly cross through this little patch of green in the midst of concrete buildings and asphalt pavement, but he seemed to be going in circles. The next street over appeared to be just a few feet away, but he never managed to reach it. His feet, like his thoughts, kept repeating the same path, over and over.

He didn't notice the three dogs running loose through the park until they were almost on top of him, snarling and growling. He broke into a run, which he soon realized to be futile, since the dogs easily ran beside him, nipping at his legs. Their slashing teeth ripped his blue jeans and they tugged hard, almost pulling him down to the ground. His lungs ached with every breath that he sucked in through his open mouth. He began to scream, even though a young man should never scream; only girls screamed. He was sure that the dogs were ripping the muscles out of his legs. He fell to the ground, certain that he was going to bleed to death, if they didn't rip out his throat first. He could feel the sticky warm fluid of his life oozing out from the bite wounds on his legs, gaping wounds that burned with pain.

The next thing he knew, his boss Martin Munt was picking him up and setting him on his feet.

"Are you alright, son?" he asked.

"I -- I think so." His voice shook as the rush of adrenalin subsided along with his fear. He still heard the pounding of his heart inside his ears.

"It's a good thing I came along when I did. People shouldn't let their dogs run loose like that. Come on, let me walk you home."

The park began to brighten up as the street lights came on, and Teddy could see strangers strolling across the grass and along the dirt paths, couples walking hand-in-hand, men in business suits seeming in a hurry to get across the park to their homes or their meetings or their happy hour at the local pub, a variety of people filling the park with their footsteps and their chatter. He saw no sign of the vicious dogs that had attacked him. Even more remarkably, he seemed to be uninjured; he must have imagined those bleeding wounds.

"You know, son," Munt said, "your mother is right."

"Right about what?"

"Now, I know that you haven't been getting along with your mother, but she really does have you best interests at heart. She's right about that girl Cindy."

"Candy," Teddy corrected him.

"Candy, Cindy, whatever her name is, she's no good for you. And you shouldn't go marrying the first girl you ever kissed."

Teddy wondered how his boss knew so much about him, but he kept silent. Perhaps Mom had a talk with Mr. Munt; yes, that must be it.

"You're new to the world, kid, and there's a lot more to experience before you get yourself tied down with all that responsibility. You're like a newborn kitten that hasn't even opened its eyes yet."

As he walked down the concrete sidewalks toward home, Teddy began to hear a reassuring feminine voice inside his head. She began telling him a story about rocket ships and men on the Moon, the death of an American President and the fall of the Soviet Union. It all seemed fantastic, like the comics in the window of the book store that he passed every day on his way to work. Except for the bug-eyed monsters and brass brassieres, which didn't seem to have any place in her story. Instead, she spoke about television signals coming from satellites in Earth orbit, telephones with no cords that you could carry in your pocket and evil entities watching him through his own eyes. When he got home, he frantically scribbled notes about everything that he could remember from her story. Television was so new that almost nobody he knew even owned a set, the expense hardly being worth it for a tiny screen that you had to look at through a magnifying lens. Telephones were big black boxes bolted to the wall, usually in the kitchen, so housewives could talk while cooking dinner. Evil entities did not exist, even if Mom did believe that such phantoms had killed her sister. It was a stroke, brought on by high blood pressure for which Marian had refused treatment, preferring to consult spiritual healers.

He began to realize that his boss and his mother were right, that he should not marry Candy. He must find the woman whose voice had spoken to him inside his head, helped him with quadratic equations and told him fantastic tales of the future. This would be his life's quest, to find her and marry her. She would save him from the terrible fate of marrying badly. In the back of his mind he felt an itch, the hint of a thought that he had another life, in another time and place, but it faded away in the mists of missing memory.

The alien slugs tried to wipe out all memory in the subject of his former life as a composer of trashy movie themes, and they became irritated when pieces of it leaked through. Obviously, they must get him out of the record store and into a job that did not involve music. He must not regain his memory until they had completed their experiment.

The next day when Teddy walked to work, his feet carried him into the book store, not the record store. He felt certain that he had walked right past the garish display of comics in the book store window and in through the front door of Magic Music, but he found himself surrounded by book shelves.

"Sorry," he said to the wrinkled old man at the cash register, and he stepped back outside.

He was certain that he had walked the ten paces down to Magic Music, but when he opened the front door he found himself inside Bentley Books again. He prayed for the feminine voice to guide him, to reassure him, but apparently her power did not reach inside this room.

"You ready?" the old man asked.

"Ready?" he stammered, "for wh- wha- what?"

"Come on, son, I'm not paying you to stand around all day. Go in the back and unpack the new arrivals. The customers can't buy them, if we don't get them out onto the shelves."

#

When the workmen broke through the door into the padded room at the amusement park, they found Robert Wells sitting in his wheelchair, his eyes staring off into space and his face expressionless.

The ambulance carried him off to the hospital, where doctors prepared him for brain surgery. His wife and daughter sat dutifully at his bedside until Edna decided that she couldn't possibly miss her bridge club, so she left Angelica sitting with her catatonic father. The orderlies took him off to some other part of the hospital for an MRI, and still Angelica waited patiently beside the empty hospital bed until they brought him back.

He lay there unresponsive, a limp hunk of flesh that seemed to have no soul behind its vacant eyes. She held her father's hand and spoke softly to him, hoping to light some spark of recognition, or at least of life, in those sunken eyes that fixed their gaze on some distant, invisible scene. She told him about her classes, her friends and her one special boyfriend, the guy who just might be the one. She kept on talking about anything at all, from the newspaper headlines to the newest theories in microbiology, hoping that her voice would reach him, somewhere deep in his unconscious mind.

She couldn't possibly know that the alien slugs were holding his mind in Limbo, watching him struggle through a computer-generated life. The alien slugs couldn't possibly know that Robert Wells was hearing everything that his daughter said, albeit in a distorted manner. They shut down the holographic display at the amusement park, since it was no longer needed, now that they had everything connected directly to the subject's mind.

When Edna Stax Wells got home, she ordered the servants to remove the hated keyboard and other equipment from her husband's bedroom and store them in the basement. She hated clutter. When they changed the bedding, they found a stack of papers under his pillows, so they took it to her. Even with her limited knowledge of musical notation, gained from a year spent studying violin in the high school orchestra class, she could see that these were not trashy movie themes. The scribbled titles alone told her that Robert had written some serious music: three symphonies, five concertos and half a dozen sonatas that might be worthy of a cultured audience. She phoned a friend at the local symphony orchestra and asked him to take a look at them.

#

Herbert Craft had urgent problems to deal with. The park's computers refused to run the demonstration program that his staff had so carefully prepared for them. He had planned to wow the guests in their formal attire with a real 1940s ballroom dance hall, complete with a mirror ball hanging from the ceiling and a big band on the stage, all created with the magic of computers and laser holograms. Instead, they milled around in a padded white room, thinking that they ought to lock up their host, who was obviously out of his mind if he thought that they were going to stick around for this kind of nonsense. It looked like a padded cell from a Hollywood movie insane asylum, and they were not inclined to stay there.

Computer programmers frantically typed at their keyboards in the control room, but the hardware refused to respond. It seemed to be under the control of some outside entity, or else it was running on its own. Somebody must have introduced a trojan virus into the software that launched its malicious code as soon as they powered up the mainframe. They did manage to get the Inferno scene back up, so they decided to run with it, that scenario being better than nothing.

Craft resolved to file a lawsuit against Wells, who had obviously damaged this attraction when he broke in, without permission, for a sneak peek at the demonstration. His wrath was somewhat soothed by the thought that somebody would have to pay for this.

By the end of the week, they had the attractions working and the amusement park open to the public. They never did find an adequate explanation for the computer glitch that had ruined the grand opening. In fact, the program had been altered to include many scenes which they had not coded. Some were parts of Dante's *Divine Comedy* which they had planned to add later, and some were little subplots whose source they didn't know. In fact, a completely new character had been added to every attraction. An adolescent boy named Teddy was walking through all of the scenarios, and they had no idea who Teddy was. Since the tourists didn't complain, they left Teddy in the program; it would have taken months of tedious work to write him out.

#

Edna Stax Wells visited her husband's hospital room once every day because it was expected of her, because it was the proper thing to do. Their daughter took the opportunity to go down to the cafeteria to eat something and to freshen up in the public restroom. Feeling that some additional help was needed, she stopped in the little chapel on the hospital's ground floor. While she was kneeling in prayer, a man in black vestment approached and stood silently in the aisle until she finished.

"Are you a priest?" she asked, gazing up at the tall, dark-complexioned man with curly dark hair.

"Of a sort. My name is Father Diep. Is there some way that I can help you?"

"Please pray for my father, Father." It sounded funny, the repetition, and she giggled a little.

Father Diep smiled. "That's what I'm here for. And to offer counseling, if you wish."

"Oh, no, not right now. I have to get back to my father's room, so he won't be alone. Mom won't stay very long. She hates hospitals."

"Don't we all?" the priest said. "But sometimes they are a necessary evil."

Edna sat in the uncomfortable bedside chair watching the nurses come and go, reading the *Chronicle*, and when she had finished the society columns, she stood up and left. She found it a great burden to waste an hour or two every day sitting beside a vegetable. That was what her husband had become, a lump of unthinking flesh. Sometimes she read the paper aloud to him, hoping that the entertainment news might spark something in his mind. Reviews of books and movies had always excited him, but now he just lay there, lost in his own world. She felt disgusted, but of course she hid that feeling and tried to act like the devoted wife that people expected her to be. It was not that she didn't care, but rather that she dared not break down. She had to be the strong one, always had to be his pillar of support. She had married a weak man who was always looking for others to rescue him, instead of buckling down and working through his own problems.

Meanwhile, the implant was spreading its tendrils deeper into her husband's brain, tapping memories and instincts of which he was not consciously aware, feeding them back to the amusement park's computer in a feedback loop that altered his experience and reprogrammed the software that displayed scenarios to park visitors. None of the spectators complained, but the subject was very palpably upset. The alien slugs tweaked the software here and there, inserting bits of code that satisfied their own sense of how the story should unfold, but they spent most of their time passively observing the show while licking the slips of green paper from the subject's wallet, which were coated with a very tasty ink, and munching on plants that they had plucked from farm fields and backyard gardens. The park visitors, who knew nothing of the alien slugs, moaned and shrieked with fear when the dogs attacked Teddy and cheered when he got a date with Candy.

#

Teddy was certain that he worked at the record store, not the book store, but he decided to play along with this game. Anyway, he had no choice. He had tried three more times to enter Magic Records, but each time he found himself inside Bentley Books, facing an old man who bore a strong resemblance to his twelfth-grade algebra instructor. The musty air smelled of dust and ink, and it made him sneeze. He hoped that it wouldn't set off one of his asthma attacks. Thinking that he must be losing his mind, he patiently pulled the new books out of their shipping boxes and placed them on the shelves, arranged alphabetically and by genre. From time to time, he found a book that some customer had replaced on the wrong shelf, so he took it to its proper place. Finding a copy of *Plato's Dialogues* among the children's books, he started to carry it to the philosophy section, when the fancy leather-bound volume slipped out of his hand.

Teddy jumped, certain that Dr. Bell would yell at him for dropping such a valuable book, but instead of hitting the ground with a thud, the book melted, blew up like a balloon and then molded itself into the form of a man wearing a toga. Teddy blinked a few times, but the man still stood there in front of him.

"Do not make my mistake, young man," Plato said.

"What mistake?" He reached out with one hand to see whether the man was real and solid or some kind of hallucination that his hand would pass right through, and Plato took his hand and shook it.

"Faith, young man. I had no faith. Of course, it wasn't my fault, since the Savior had not yet appeared, which is why I'm stuck here in Limbo and not in some pit of torture. But I can never move up higher, as you can. All it takes is a mustard seed of faith."

"I don't know what you're talking about," Teddy said, "but you are supposed to be on the shelf with the other philosophy books."

"Books? Do I look like a book? Look at me, boy!"

Teddy studied the man who stood before him, a very small man, certainly not an inch over five feet, with his hair cut short on the sides and back, with long curls around his brow. The man was barefoot, and in his toga he looked almost girlish, except for the hawk nose and dark, piercing eyes that marked him as decidedly masculine. Plato looked directly into his eyes and seemed to detect all his most jealously guarded secrets.

"But you were a book! I held you in my hand, I dropped you, and then --"

"Shadows," the little man said.

"What?"

"You see only the shadows of the real objects. Things are not as they appear. Things are never as they appear."

"Well, considering what just happened, I guess I ought to agree."

"Very good! You have just taken the first step toward wisdom. Your body might be tied to the chair, your gaze fixed on the wall of the cave, your sight shrouded in darkness, but your mind can set you free."

"Excuse me, sir, but what are you talking about?"

"Truth, young man! The first step toward the truth is to admit that you don't know anything."

"Okay, so I don't know anything. What of it?"

"The next step is faith, boy! We pagans are stuck here in Limbo, never able to approach Paradise, since we never knew the Savior. But you, and others as fortunate as you, have the opportunity to approach the light of God himself."

"I don't believe you," Teddy protested. "Larry must have put something funny in my coffee this morning. You can't be real."

As if in agreement, the little man dissolved and fell to the floor with a thud. He was once again a leather-bound book of *Plato's Dialogues* with gilt lettering on the spine and the front cover. Teddy picked it up and slid it into its proper place in the philosophy section.

Walking home at the end of the day, Teddy thought that he really ought to buy himself a car. He had seen an old used Hudson Terraplane for sale, a cute sporty coupe with an automatic clutch, which had been the latest in modern technology back in 1939. To shift gears, you pushed buttons on the dashboard. The car's black paint still shone like new under a thick coat of highly buffed wax. It was used, but it looked to be in good condition, and it was only fifty dollars. In his present financial condition however, it might as well be fifty thousand dollars. Maybe his mother would lend him the money, but he knew that she would insist that he move back home. The thought depressed him; he had been feeling overwhelmed lately. Even before he found himself in the bookstore, and before the little man talked all that nonsense, he had felt odd, as if he were not quite right in the head. Besides, Candy had decided to date other men, so he had broken up with her and now felt regret as a whirlpool inside his belly, sucking his soul into the abyss. He let his feet do the steering, and he found himself not on the little street where his mother lived, and not heading toward Larry's big house where he rented a room, but somewhere downtown on a bridge over a river.

Leaning over the rail, he watched the muddy water flowing by, boiling around a rotting log, lapping at the concrete banks. He couldn't remember ever having been here before, and he thought that he knew every bit of his home town. He began to feel the urge to jump over the rail, leap into the water and end it all right here, before he completely lost his mind. Before he could tell his legs to climb on top of the rail, however, he became suddenly dizzy and lightheaded, and then he fell down in a faint.

#

Chapter Five

Teddy's high school classmate Bobby came home from Korea without his left leg. He spoke of beautiful green hills and rice paddies stretching to the horizon, and he spoke of the stifling dust and heat, the soaking rains, the pelting storm of bullets and the shells dropping out of the sky. He did not speak of how he lost his leg; he could not remember anything but the enormous pain that he felt upon waking up in the MASH unit. His left leg still hurt him, even though it had been cut off below the knee. He hobbled around on crutches, wearing civilian clothes. The uniform, which his mother lovingly packed away in the attic, had won him only scorn and derision from a public that did not understand, ignorant people who blamed the soldier for the war. When strangers asked Bobby what happened to his leg, he said that he had been hit by a train. In a way, that was true. The whole Korean conflict had become a huge international train wreck. Truman had come within a hair's breadth of ordering nuclear bombs to be dropped, just like Hiroshima and Nagasaki.

Teddy envied Bobby for his rugged good looks, slicked back dark hair and a face that reminded him of Clark Gable. But that jealous feeling shattered on the ground when Teddy's gaze fell to the stump where Bobby's leg used to be. The girls swooned when they saw him, but he couldn't take them out dancing any more. Bobby refused all sympathy, referring to his comrades who never came home, those who had fallen down on Horseshoe Ridge and never stood up again. He spent his days sitting in his wheelchair on the front lawn of his mother's house, turning into an old man before his time.

The radio told news of the war, and the newspapers went into more depth. Before the main feature at the Gem movie theater, newsreels showed the propaganda clips. All of it gave Teddy a queasy feeling, as if he had been there himself, even though his medical condition had spared him the draft.

From the bare hills of Pusan in the south, to the pine-covered mountains in the north, American soldiers answered the call of the United Nations to stop the assault of Communist North Korea upon the democratic nation of South Korea, both countries filled with short, slant-eyed people with straight black hair and dark skin, dressed all in black, with long-sleeved tunics and loose-fitting pants tied around their waists with cords. The troops engaged in a holding action, waiting for the international forces to come in and take over. The holding action went on month after month, and still the majority of the forces holding back the Communists from the north were American, with a few British troops helping out. The conflict dragged on for three years, and the authorities still refused to call it a war.

When General MacRobert was called home, the newscasters wept. How could President Truman treat the great hero of World War Two so shabbily? After some alarming talk of using the atomic bomb, they declared a cease-fire, not a truce or a treaty or even an end to the war, since they never agreed to call it a war.

Bobby had nightmares about the battle, about his fellow soldiers falling to the ground, pieces of their shattered bodies flying everywhere, landing everywhere, bits of flesh and bone and gore speckling his face. When the President made an extemporaneous remark about "nucular" weapons, Bobby wished that they would use the nukes on North Korea and on Communist China, to wipe the inhuman torturers off the face of the planet. He had seen the civilians, victims of the advancing Communist troops, some dismembered so badly that they lay dead in the streets, others walking wounded with missing limbs and disfigured faces. He hated the Communists with a passion, so he could not understand when Teddy joined a Socialist student group, and he broke off their friendship. Teddy was taking a night class in political science at the University of California, Berkeley, where the course work and class discussions reinforced his anti-war sentiments and leftist leanings.

He had recurring nightmares in which he found himself among the American forces south of the 38th parallel with the North Korean Army advancing toward them behind an unrelenting shower of artillery. Soviet tanks escorted the enemy troops while YAK fighters harassed the Americans from the air. As a peace-keeping force, the American units had little armor and air support to back up the sadly deficient South Korean Army. The onslaught rolled over Teddy's prone body in his nightmares, and he floated above his body to a great height where he could see the enemy troops marching all the way to Pusan in the south, crushing buildings and people alike under their boots and tank treads. He awoke covered with sweat, screaming in horror. He felt afraid, not only for himself, but for the world that might any day be shredded into tatters by the atomic bombs which mad scientists had developed during the Second War to End All Wars. Finding that he could not focus his eyes, he closed them again and fell back into a fitful sleep.

#

In Plato's "Allegory of the Cave", we find ourselves seated in a cave, looking at the back wall. We are tied up so that we cannot turn around and look back at the entrance to the cave, where people are walking by while carrying various objects that cast shadows onto the wall. Even if we did manage to turn around, the sunlight would blind us, so that we could not see anything outside of the cave. We are trapped in a faux reality where we see only the shadows of the real things that exist outside of our awareness, and even if somebody untied you and dragged you outside, you would be as blind as an owl in daylight.

Since owls are nocturnal creatures, they have very large eyes with extreme sensitivity to low light levels. In bright light, the pupil closes down to a pinpoint to protect the retina, which is packed with light-sensitive rods. Many species also have a reflective layer behind the retina, called the tapetum lucidum, which reflects back onto the rods any light that might have passed through the retina without hitting one the first time Although they have fewer light sensitive cones than humans, they probably can detect some colors. Technically, owls are not blind in daylight, but humans can see better at night than owls can during the day.

#

When they brought Rob Wells back from his MRI, he was still unconscious. He had an IV feeding antibiotics into his left arm to fight an infection that had caused a high fever. He occasionally mumbled something unintelligible, but he never opened his eyes or gave any sign of awareness of his surroundings. Angelica sat by her father's bedside all evening, but at nine o'clock the nurse told her that she had to leave, since visiting hours were over. She drove home in her little Toyota, and the big mansion seemed like an empty shell without her father's music to fill it up.

The alien slugs pondered the chatter of their subject's female attendants, having no clear understanding of family relationships and regarding the wife and daughter as servants who attended his bedside when the nurses were busy at their station. They wisely decided not to let the females' speech filter back into the computer, since the people at the amusement park might catch on to the game and try to put a stop to it. They might even shut down the computer, putting an end to the game before they had finished their study.

The implant was running out of battery power, so they decided to use brute force on the program by putting their subject under severe stress to see what kind of decisions he would make.

#

In the Church of the Unknown God, the priests were conducting the High Mass. Mother Iris in robes of white with gold braid trim recited prayers over the table that was laid out with the wine and the host, while Brother Densing in robes of scarlet with silver trim walked down the aisle with the censer hanging from brass chains, filling the air with the warm, edgy fragrance of frankincense. Father Diep stood to one side of the table, waiting for Mother Iris to finish and give him leave to participate in the distribution of the holy sacraments to the congregation. The liturgical music from the pipe organ rose to an almost deafening crescendo, then gradually diminished to the level of ambience.

Father Diep loved the spectacle of the Mass. It filled his heart with what the early Church Fathers used to call Enthusiasm, or the indwelling of the Holy Spirit. He sincerely believed that theatre was good for the soul. He found the music especially elevating. The organized tones and rhythms seemed to clear his thoughts as no other mechanism could.

On his own time, when he made his private prayers, he included Robert Wells, a composer of powerful music. He had heard about the mugging on the television news, had gone to Queen of the Valley hospital to pray for Wells in their little chapel, had even met the man's daughter. All of this he did at the calling of an inner voice, as if it were his personal mission to save the soul of a man he never had met.

Father Diep had seen some of the movies that Robert Wells had graced with his scores. He had a great interest in demonology, and even a cheap thriller usually added something to his understanding of the rite of exorcism. That was how he had become acquainted with the brilliant compositions with their elevating ambience, the kind of music that might be played in a church, rather than to enhance a monster movie. He believed that the composer put a piece of his soul into every note, every rhythm.

He had discussed this with his Father Confessor, who submitted to the church hierarchy and attained approval for his adoption of a personal mission to pray for Robert Wells. He used his prayer time to ask the Lord to intervene, to allow him to enter the mind of the composer who now lay in a coma, to help him awaken and recover.

#

Herbert Craft used the scene where Faust conjured up the devil to introduce Dante's *Inferno*, even though the two works came from different eras, centuries apart. He cared more for dramatic effect than for historical accuracy. He loved watching the gray-bearded figure of Faust, dressed in a flowing robe with white stars and crescent moons on a dark blue background, casting spells, intoning magical phrases in the German language and tossing chemical powders into the fire, watching them erupt in colorful bursts. "Erschein!" sounded so much more forceful than the English equivalent, "Appear!" Faust began his routine by picking up the Holy Bible and stashing it under his bench, then opening a book of spells that would lead him to damnation. Craft liked the fact that Goethe left room for Faust's redemption at the end, just when the demons from Hell were about to drag him down through the floor of his dimly lit chamber. Cheating the Devil was a good thing, in his opinion.

Dante divided the afterlife into three regions: Paradise, Purgatory and Inferno. When Robert Wells first entered the empty white room at the amusement park, he had accidentally tripped the switch that started up the Inferno presentation. The more familiar name for it was Hell. Dante divided his Inferno into nine circles, but for the sake of time and simplicity, the park's computers sent visitors immediately to the fiery pit, which Herbert Craft had considered the most shocking part of Dante's description of the underworld. Of course he showed them the familiar scenes that high school students read about: Sisyphus pushing a huge boulder up a hill, only to have it roll back down, over and over; Tantalus standing in a pool of water that ran away every time he tried to take a drink, and with a bunch of grapes above his head that rose higher whenever he reached up to take some; and Orpheus and Eurydice, two lovers torn apart by the winds of Hell. He also played the music from classical operas on these subjects for the visitors to hear, thinking that they might acquire some veneer of culture from the experience.

Dante's *Inferno* showed the opportunists, who did no good and no evil, stuck between Hell and Purgatory, chasing a banner along the shores of a river and being stung by hornets as a symbol of the sting of conscience. Craft thought it too boring to include in his presentation. The highest circle of Hell contained the virtuous pagans in a sort of counterfeit Paradise or Heaven. He included a snippet of that first circle only to lead the visitors into the story of judgment, with King Minos sitting just outside that first circle and condemning souls to the lower circles of Hell, where they would suffer eternal damnation and punishment for their sins. The programmers hadn't completed the software for Purgatory and Paradise, so he planned to introduce them later, when people had grown bored with his park and he would need something new to keep the paying customers coming in.

The Purgatory attraction would be a bare bones affair, leading into the vision of Paradise with Beatrice, Dante's vision of beauty and inspiration, looking down on the travelers as they strove upward. He thought that Beatrice sounded too old-fashioned and corny, so Craft changed her name to something more enchanting. After trying several names that didn't quite fit, he settled upon Lorelei, the beautiful goddess who lures sailors to their death by singing to them and luring them closer and closer, until they smash their boats upon the rocks. Somehow, Craft had always suspected that Paradise was an evil illusion.

They had finished programming Mozart's *The Magic Flute*, and Craft had enjoyed it so much that he visited it six times before the ribbon cutting ceremony. His favorite character was Papageno, the chubby little bird catcher who found himself covered with feathers and chirping like a bird. He was a much more interesting fellow than handsome, boring Prince Tamino, who passed through tests by playing a flute that charmed men and beasts, while little Papageno actually took risks, even if he did sometimes resort to ringing his magic bells to distract his enemies. Besides, Tamino knew all along that his prize would be marriage to the beautiful Princess Pamina, while Papageno was given an old hag who only became young and beautiful after he agreed to marry her. Sometimes Craft wished that he could be Papageno. Other times, he wished that he could be Faust, the great magician who conjured up the Devil and made him do his bidding.

#

In the early versions of the Faust legend, a highly educated Doctor of Divinity conjures up the Devil and lives a life of luxury and debauchery for twenty years. At the end of that time, however, he must fulfill his end of the bargain, the contract that he signed in his own blood. In Christopher Marlowe's version, for example, he hides in the basement of his house, but the demons find him there, tear his body to shreds and drag his soul down into the depths of Hell. Johan Wilhelm von Goethe, writing in the Romantic era, found this ending too horrible, so he changed it. Believing that Christ can save any soul, no matter how damned, he had God tell the Devil that the contract was null and void because Faust had been tricked into performing his role in a scenario that was created to play out a wager between God and the Devil. Beside, he didn't really get Helen of Troy, but only a demon transformed to look like the most beautiful woman in the world. The Devil had fudged on the deal, so the contract was broken. Thus, the story of Faust was transformed into the story of Plato's cave. Goethe's Faust was as blind to the truth as an owl in daylight.

#

Teddy was not surprised to find himself on the field of battle, but he was perplexed to find his boss from the bookstore, Dr. Bell, trudging along beside him. He wondered how the old man could keep up with him, since they were carrying full packs weighing seventy-five pounds. Teddy barely managed to carry the weight himself, and he thought that he couldn't stand another minute of the frost-laden wind slashing his fingers and face in this Korean winter night. The shelling from the enemy lines brought welcome light and heat, along with the intended death and destruction. He felt a deep sadness when he realized that the landscape was littered with the dead and dying from both sides. The silence of the dead sounded worse than the moans of the dying. Sniper fire harassed the American troops, changing Teddy's attitude toward the bursts of light that made him visible to the enemy while making the gruesome scene visible to him . He wondered whether he could fire the rifle that he carried, whether he could aim at another human being, even an enemy whose job it was to kill him. Honor and duty to his country demanded that he shoot and kill, but his legs turned rubbery at the thought. He kept marching, and Dr. Bell stayed beside him, through snow and darkness and terror. Up ahead, they heard a man screaming. As they approached the sound, an occasional flash from an exploding shell illuminated a young soldier lying on the ground, trying to shove his guts back into his belly.

"He filled his belly in life," Dr. Bell said, "at the expense of others."

"So this is the punishment for his sin?" Teddy asked. "What kind of God could allow such torture?"

"He is punishing himself. It's all in his mind."

"It's in my mind, too, and I can't stand it. Am I being punished, too?"

"Not punished, educated. Enlightened."

"Why?"

"So you will know and understand."

"But why me?"

Dr. Bell sighed and shrugged, and then he said, "Why not you?"

They walked on through the night, across the rice paddy and over a hill, until they had left the field of battle behind. Dr. Bell showed no sign of fatigue, but Teddy was so worn out that he sat down on the muddy, half-frozen ground and shrugged the pack off of his back. A winter storm blew the sharp-edged snowflakes unrelentingly, so he pulled the strings on his hood tighter to cover as much of his face as possible. Dr. Bell stood beside him as if the snow and wind and cold did not affect him.

"You have much to learn," he said, shrugging off his backpack. The figure of the old man in a pin-striped business suit, carrying a full military pack, looked incongruous in these surroundings.

"I graduated high school. That's all the education I need." He shivered.

"You feel the cold because your eyes see the storm. Look beyond what you see."

"What's that supposed to mean?"

"Just look."

Teddy looked up at the sky, a whited-out expanse of overcast that hid the stars and blurred the light of the full moon into a smear of white light among the storm clouds. He thought that he saw black snowflakes flitting across the horizon, five or six of them, blacker than the night. Snowflakes are white, he told himself, but he saw these black forms approaching from the west. At first he thought that they were missiles, but they did not move in a straight course. They turned in circles, going higher and lower, gradually approaching his position like spiraling trails of crepe paper party favors. He shook his head and rubbed his eyes, but the black forms kept coming toward him, growing larger and taking the shape of human bodies. As they came within a few hundred feet, he could hear them screaming.

"Why are they being punished?"

"Lust. The punishment for lust is the winds of Hell." Oddly, Dr. Bell seemed to have traded his pin-striped suit for the black vestments of a priest.

"Is it all in their minds? Are they punishing themselves?"

"Of course they are. They have a lesson to learn, and a lesson to teach you. Pay attention."

Watching the sky, Teddy observed the damned creatures tossed by the wind, spinning and screaming. Presently, they began to hold hands with each other, forming letters in the sky, letters formed by the shapes of their bodies. Fascinated, Teddy watched them spell out, 'THE TRUTH SHALL SET YOU FREE".

Dr. Bell walked away, and Teddy called after him, but the old man kept on walking. Afraid to be left alone in this eerie landscape, Teddy forced himself to stand up and follow him. Teddy noticed that both of their packs lay in the mud, left behind like dead soldiers. They trudged though filthy muck up to their ankles, crossing the remains of a battle-stricken rice paddy, while the stormy night folded itself around their shoulders. Teddy never had felt so cold and forlorn in his life.

He kept praying silently that the feminine voice would come back to guide him out of this horrible place, but all that he could hear was the sound of bells, like sleigh bells. Yes. there must be a horse and sleigh somewhere nearby, and he thought that perhaps he could hitch a ride. Scanning the horizon, he searched in vain for the horse and sleigh that must be approaching. His feet grew heavier with each step, making a sucking sound as he pulled them up out of the muck and then sliding around as he sought to gain purchase on the slimy surface.

"Put those bells away," the old man said. "The enemy can hear them."

Then Teddy realized that he was carrying a leather strap across his shoulders, and attached to that strap were a dozen silvery metal bells tinkling away. He dropped it on the ground, but it leaped back onto his shoulders. Three times he tossed it down, and three times it leaped back up.

":Fold it up and put it in your pocket, boy!"

Teddy obeyed, folding up the strap and wondering how he would ever fit something that big inside his pocket, when a shell landed right in front of them, bursting with fire and shock, blowing the two men into bits of blood and bone and gore. As he felt his limbs being torn from his body, he could hear the old man saying, "It's all in your mind, boy."

#

Chapter Six

The next day Robert Wells' fever had gone down, but the doctors still felt that he was not well enough to tolerate the surgery to remove his brain tumor. Angelica spent a few hours with her father, but then she told him that she had to get back to school. Hoping that he would hear and understand her through the mind-numbing clouds of his coma, she told him that the doctors and nurses were doing everything they could, that he was getting the best of care, and that she promised to come and visit every Saturday.

Edna came in to spend some time with her husband, and this time she had wonderful news to tell him. She prayed that, somewhere deep in his unconscious mind, he could hear what she was telling him, even though he did not seem to respond.

"Your new music is creating quite a stir. The Boston symphony is going to perform your *Symphony of the Birds*. They consider it an artistic triumph of beauty and power and, well, when the reviews come out, I'll read them to you. Unless, of course, you're well and able to read them for yourself. They're already saying that you might be the greatest musical genius of our time."

Her husband lay still in the bed, staring at the ceiling with empty eyes, but Edna suspected the he might have heard her. She grabbed his hand and quickly squeezed it, then said, "I have to leave now, but I'll be back tomorrow. There's a little recital of your "Bell" sonata at the local symphony, and they just begged me to attend."

The alien slugs congratulated each other by slapping tentacles. They had at least succeeded in teaching the subject to create real music. He had even found a way to meld the keys of B and C into the same piece of music, directing the strings to play in B with five sharps, while the woodwinds played in C with none. They had begun to doubt that he was capable of learning the more important lessons. He showed a marked tendency to grab whatever opportunity happened to present itself, rather than planning and working toward a goal. In fact, he often seemed to expect the females to do all of his work for him, while he pursued instant gratification of his physical and emotional cravings.

#

Father Diep began to experience strange dreams, nightmares in which he was leading a teenage boy through a dreadful battlefield filled with the corpses of the dead and the screams of the dying. The weirdest part of the dream was that he was a white man; that made him feel extremely uncomfortable. Demons flew through the air as if to attack them, and indeed missiles landed all around them, bursting into clouds of shrapnel that shredded their bodies until nothing was left but their component atoms. When he awoke in a feverish sweat, the sun hadn't come up yet. It was only four o'clock in the morning. He prayed to the Unknown God for the strength to bear this burden and for the wisdom to help his new disciple along the path to understanding. Surely the seed had been planted, and now it needed water and sunlight. Surely these were more than dreams, more than the fantasy of a sleeping brain. On some level, they were more real than his waking life.

He recited the Our Father and the Beatitudes, and even the Apostles Creed, then turned on the lamp on his beside table, opened his Bible and read aloud through all of the Psalms, but still his mind was troubled, as was his heart. He sensed that a new Awakening was about to take place, but he also sensed that the forces of Evil were at work to keep the people asleep, unaware of the Truth that might set them free.

The ancients had known that this world is an illusion, that our vision is clouded because we have sinned and fallen from grace. Modern sensibilities, however, had twisted that literal truth into a metaphor, a mere poetic device. When the age of the machine divorced the common people from the land that gave them life, they became automatons with no direct connection to the Soul of the world. The Church emphasized the need to plant a garden, even if it was nothing more than a window box in a third-floor apartment. This was to remind the people of the Garden from which all humanity had been banished, and to plant the seed of Faith in their hearts, that they might gain strength and wisdom from the Living God, the Unknown God who loved them and cared for them.

In the concrete and asphalt city, where living things were relegated to parks and preserves, it was difficult to find their connection to the natural world which provided refreshment and renewal to the Soul.

#

Teddy found himself lying under water, gurgling but never quite drowning, while men and women with swords danced around his body, fighting each other. When he thought he couldn't take it any more, he fell through the ground to a lower level, where he saw dead people in their coffins, with the lids open and flames licking around their faces. He told himself that this must be Hell, and that he must find a way to escape, but his legs hung limp and useless. A masculine voice inside his head said, "The punishment for heresy." The faces in the coffins emitted piercing shrieks of pain and terror. Throwing his hands up over his face, he screamed, and then he fell again. This time he found himself standing in front of a doorway that was blocked by a huge man with the head of a bull. He almost laughed at the thought that a guard was thought necessary to keep him outside the room, whose walls and floor were made of red bricks, and where thousands of people were standing in a pool of boiling blood, thousands more were stuck to thorn bushes, and still more were standing in hot desert sands with fire raining from the sky. He covered his ears to protect them from the violence of their screams. "Yes," the masculine voice said inside his head, "They were violent in life."

Suddenly, a winged monster appeared, grabbed him with a clawed forepaw and set him onto its back. This creature had the body of a lion, with the head and wings of an eagle. Before he could hop down or yell in protest, the creature soared into the air and descended a steep cliff into a valley where souls were suffering a variety of inhuman torments, some whipped by demons, others slogging through pits of excrement, still others bitten by snakes, and more. The stench was almost as horrifying as the screams of the damned. Teddy fainted.

#

When he awoke from his fainting spell, Teddy found himself in his own bed in his own room in Larry's boarding house, with no memory of how he had gotten home from the bridge over the river. He had the vague impression that he had dreamed about war, but that was all he could dredge up from his foggy memory. The sheets and blankets were tossed into a heap on the floor and he had the dim memory of a nightmare. Seeing that it was morning, he got up and dressed for work. He had begun looking forward to seeing the derelict along the way; every time Teddy saw him, the cardboard sign had a different message. Today it was "SOPHIA IS ABOUT TO RETURN". Teddy wondered who Sophia was; perhaps the derelict had a wife or daughter with that name. He would have asked the old man, but he was too frightened of his mad, flashing eyes.

Days blended into weeks with no further incidents, except that he seemed to be working at Bentley Books now, instead of Magic Music. Larry had left his job there to become managing editor at a prestigious publishing house. Perhaps to spite his mother, or perhaps for sheer enjoyment, Teddy spent his lunch hours reading the gaudy-covered fantasy magazines with their stories of space ships and bug-eyed monsters, half-naked women and the heroes who rescued them from a fate worse than death. The feminine voice came back for a short visit once in a while and told him stories that seemed to come right out of the pages of those lurid pulp magazines. He made notes on scraps of paper that he used for page markers when he had to put down the magazines and get back to work. It wasn't long before Dr. Bell came across some of his notes and remarked about them.

"You ought to write some stories, boy. Finish them and submit them to the magazines. You might make a few extra bucks."

Blushing Teddy replied, "Oh, I'm not good enough."

"Good enough? Why, most of the stories in those magazines are not good enough. They're written by hacks who never read more than a gum wrapper in their lives. Go for it, boy, you have a talent for storytelling."

When Teddy protested that he didn't even have a typewriter, Dr. Bell led him into the office in the back of the bookstore. There on a beat-up wooden desk sat a Hermes portable typewriter, covered with dust but otherwise in good condition. The tiny room's musty smell and the annoying clutter did not appeal to him, but the typewriter did. He touched the keyboard lightly, lovingly, and told himself that he could clean up the room, even if he couldn't make it bigger. He would have to overcome his claustrophobia, but opening up new worlds in his stories might help him to ignore the cramped quarters.

"Any time you want to write," he said, "you come back here and sit down. There's a whole ream of paper and a new reel of inked ribbon in the drawer. Any time." With a wink, he pulled a ring of keys out of his pocket. Fiddling with the key ring, he pulled off one key and handed it to Teddy. "This opens the front door, in case you feel the inspiration to write when the store is closed."

One evening he took his notes into the back room and typed a story about cats coming from a distant galaxy to recruit a human to open their canned food. The alien cats were unable to work the can opener because they lacked opposable thumbs. Six weeks later, the story came back with a form rejection letter. He wrote another story about bug-eyed monsters landing on the Earth and declaring it devoid of life because they had chosen the heart of Death Valley for their landing spot. Another six weeks passed, and the story came back with another form rejection letter. There were only three magazines where he could send his fantasy fiction, so he sent each story to all three, one at a time, and they kept coming back with form rejection letters. Dr. Bell continued to encourage him, and the feminine voice continued telling him stories, so he continued writing.

Every evening he rolled a sheet of clean white paper into the platen of the Hermes portable typewriter, placed his hand on the keys and picked out the letters with three fingers on each hand, using his thumbs to press the space bar. He never had learned to type with all his fingers, the way he saw the secretaries in offices do it. But he managed well enough, and soon he was placing his manuscript lovingly into a manila envelope, writing out the address of *Amazing Stories*, licking the stamps and pasting them onto the upper right-hand corner of the envelope. He felt a sense of accomplishment for having written each story, but he longed for an acceptance, publication and a check. He must have more income, if he was going to marry Candy and support her. She still resisted him, but at least she had allowed him to take her out dancing on Saturday nights.

The alien slugs disapproved of the trash that he was writing, so they developed a scheme to put a stop to it. They entered some new parameters into the implant's software program to discourage the subject from producing hollow entertainment. Their experiment was designed to bring out great art, not lurid fantasies; not that they objected to fantasy fiction per se, but they wanted to see him produce more ambitious stories with profound meaning.

Finally, his story about a tourist sneaking into the inner sanctum of an ancient temple and finding the star drive from an alien spacecraft did not come back. Instead, he opened the mail box one Saturday morning and found an envelope containing an acceptance letter and a check for fifty dollars, enough to buy a used car or rent his own place. His first thought was to run to Candy's house and show her the check. First he ran up to his room and put on his sports jacket, and then he slicked down his thick brown hair with a comb and Brill Cream. He had to look nice for his girl, even if she wasn't technically his girl any more.

Candy's mother let him into the front room, where he sat on the edge of the sofa and waited for Candy to come down. After a few minutes, she floated into the room like a dream of chiffon and perfume, sat beside him and even touched his hand. He felt a thrill running through his spine.

"You wanted to show me something?" she asked.

Speechless, Teddy handed her the envelope that he had torn open at home twenty minutes earlier.

Candy slowly and carefully pulled out the letter and unfolded it, inspecting the message of congratulations and the check that it held. "Why, that's very nice, Teddy. Do you think your little stories could make enough money to support a wife and children?"

That one word, "little", stung him. There was nothing little about his stories. They had become the biggest thing in his life, consuming his every spare moment and occupying his mind while he performed his daily tasks, from brushing his teeth to fulfilling his duties at the book store. "Don't you understand? I'm a published author. That makes me a real artist, and not just a kid who works in a bookstore. I'm going to be famous."

"You mean," Candy said, drawing out each word slowly and with a critical slant of her eyebrows, "you put your real name on that trash?" Her voice remained sweet, but her words cut him. "Why, everybody will know that *you* wrote that garbage."

Teddy ran out of the room, out of the house and down the sidewalk. Stumbling home, he told himself that he was through with Candy, really through this time. When he got home, he turned on the Magnavox and listened to the radio broadcast of classical music on high volume. Strauss' *Also Sprach Zarathustra* was playing when Larry came in from his errands with two brown bags of groceries in his arms. Teddy jumped up and helped carry them into the kitchen. A couple decades later, that music would become the theme for a movie called *2001*, but Teddy knew nothing about the future. He still didn't understand that the feminine voice was telling him about true future events.

Larry, always cheerful, glanced at Teddy's face and asked, "Something got you down?"

"What?"

"Turn down the radio, so you can hear me."

Teddy obeyed and then returned to the kitchen, where Larry was setting out eggs, cheese and a variety of produce on the counter.

"What's wrong?"

"Nothing."

"It's a girl, isn't it?"

"Yeah," Teddy admitted.

"The Frigidaire needs cleaning. Come on and help me; it'll take your mind off of your problems." The lean blond man reached out with delicate artist's fingers and pulled open the latch on the refrigerator door.

They pulled everything out and sorted it into piles of garbage and stacks of keepers. A brick of what used to be cheddar cheese was now covered with rosettes of blue-green mold. A head of iceberg lettuce had turned into a small lump of slime. Pulling out a tray of hamburger that smelled of death and rot, Larry said, "This thing is about to grow legs and walk away." Chuckling at his own joke, he slid out the fruit bin and stuck it under the faucet, rinsed it out with hot water and turned it upside down on the counter to drip dry.

Using a claw hammer and a table knife, Teddy chinked away at the slabs of frost in the freezer, a process that the manufacturer strongly disapproved, as it could break the coils and ruin their magnificent machine. They were supposed to leave the freezer door open for three hours and wait for the frost to melt, but who had that kind of patience? Besides, their ice cream would melt and their food could thaw out and go bad in three hours.

Larry tried to engage him in conversation while they worked, but Teddy's mind kept wandering to what

Candy had said, how she had disapproved of his first great triumph as a writer. Then he thought of the gentle feminine voice that told him the stories and encouraged him to write them. She hadn't spoken to him in weeks, maybe months; he couldn't remember exactly how long, but he was painfully aware that her absence created an empty spot in his life, a hole that threatened to swallow him up.

"You've been chewing your nails," Larry observed. "Mom used to paint my fingers with tincture of iodine, and it put a stop to that nasty habit. Do you want me to get a bottle of iodine?"

Teddy smiled a little and shook his head no, but he was glad that somebody cared about him. He pulled out the envelope that he had stuck into his back pocket and handed it to Larry.

"Why, you've sold a story! That's fantastic! You're going to be published, so why are you so sad?"

"Candy called it garbage. She said my story was trash."

"Who cares what Candy says? Is she an editor? No. A publisher? No. Why, she isn't even a writer."

Teddy still cared, but he did feel a little bit better.

"Let's go to the museum, and when we get back I'll make one of my infamous soufflés."

Teddy, who rarely felt hungry and almost never ate anything but a few soda crackers, could easily be enticed into eating one of Larry's masterpieces. The delicate flavors and textures of his artistic kitchen productions went far beyond mere provender.

Teddy had thought that Larry was taking him to the art museum, but instead they went to the University's Museum of Paleontology to look at dinosaurs and Ice Age mammals. They pulled up in front of the Hearst Memorial Mining Building where the exhibits were housed, a rectangular structure with the appearance of an ancient monument due to the triple arches in the façade before the entrance. That appearance was deceptive. The building consisted of three square stucco buildings connected to each other in their interiors, but topped with separate Spanish tile roofs, with the central building some six feet taller than the two on the sides. Despite the early twentieth-century style of the construction, something about it reminded them of a medieval castle. Going through the front door, they felt as if they were entering a mausoleum.

First they strolled through the central hall where a Columbian mammoth's bones had been wired together and propped up with steel supports, its tusks curling forward from its jaws. The beast was huge, almost too big for the building to house it. Then they looked at the display of aquatic reptiles from Ichthyosaur State Park near Berlin, Nevada, creatures shaped like a cross between an alligator and a fish. Several skeletons were wired together and placed on iron stands, bare bones posed as if in life, and artist's conceptions of what they looked like with flesh and skin hung on the wall.

"They're all gone," Larry said. "Dead, extinct. I should write a poem about them."

They're scary," Teddy said.

"Aw, you frighten too easily. They can't hurt you, they're dead."

They moved on, looking at fossils from New Mexico, Oregon and Nevada, the bones of fantastic creatures that might have inspired tales of dragons and sea monsters. A log from the Petrified Forest turned out to be as heavy as a rock when they tried, and failed, to lift it. They looked at stuffed specimens of modern animals, mostly bears from Alaska. The brown Kodiak bear standing upright and the white polar bear posed on all fours certainly looked like prehistoric giants, so it was hard to believe that they were still living today. They moved on to the museum's collection of bones from bizarre extinct mammals found in the tar pits of Rancho La Brea, way down south in Los Angeles. There were a few bones of early man in that exhibit, testifying that people had walked among the strange beasts and that people had fallen into the sticky tar, never to escape.. The skeleton of a giant ground sloth had been wired together and posed standing up beside an artificial tree, as if it were reaching up with its muzzle to chew the leaves on low-hanging branches. Bird skeletons hung from wires in the ceiling, perched on artificial tree branches, while aquatic birds sat in imaginary pools of water. Wolf-like creatures harassed goat-like herbivores. The exhibits of skeletons were augmented by artists' sketches, complete with fur and feathers, on the walls.

"This is your lucky day," Larry said. "They keep the tar pit fossils in the Sather Tower on the campus, and they almost never bring them here for people to see."

Teddy, who had been following his friend around in a mental fog produced by the tacit rejection he had received from Candy, suddenly found himself face to face with the skull of a Smilodon, a saber-toothed cat. It was bigger than the lions at the zoo, and its canine teeth stuck out like backward tusks from its jowls.

Either from hunger or from fright, he passed out on the spot.

Teddy came back to awareness and found himself sitting near a camp fire at night, surrounded by primitive people dressed in animal skins. He was surprised to find himself dressed in the same garb. He opened his mouth to speak, but all that came out were guttural sounds like those of a deaf man. The others seemed to think that he was asking for food, since they handed him baskets filled with bits of dried meat, nuts and berries. A huge cat, some kind of pet, prowled among them until one of them tossed it a thigh bone covered with half-cooked meat. Apparently, the day's hunt had gone well. The cat settled down to chew its meal, and Teddy saw that it was a saber-tooth, but not wild or frightening at all. It was as tame as any housecat. He thought that he heard one of the men saying, "It's all in your mind," but then he was distracted by the sight of a topless, half-naked woman approaching him with another basket of food. His youthful hormones raged.

He reached out to take the basket and found himself suddenly inside a cage made of iron bars. A huge mulatto stood nearby, and the presence of another human being soothed his jangled nerves.

"Where am I?" he asked.

The big man laughed.

"For Christ's sake, tell me where I am!"

He chuckled softly this time, and he spoke with a tenderness in his voice. "I am so sorry, but you have asked me that same question twelve times already. Will you please try to remember the answer this time?"

"I'll do my best." Teddy began rubbing the back of his head, where he felt a painful knot from some blow that he must have taken.

"You are under the Coliseum, in Rome, waiting to go forth and show your courage."

"You mean, they're going to throw me to the lions?"

"No, that is what we do to Christians and other heretics. You are a gladiator, capable of winning your life and perhaps your freedom, if you fight bravely and win the favor of the Emperor."

His heart sank. He was no warrior, no kind of fighter. His knees buckled as the soldiers dragged him out of his cage and shoved a sword into his hand, then led him through the dark, damp tunnel of limestone blocks, out into the blinding sunlight. He fell on his face.

The next thing he knew, Larry was picking him up and shaking him. "I didn't know you spoke Latin."

"I don't."

"But you were speaking it. Conversational Latin, as if you had spoken it all your life."

"That's spooky. Let's get out of here."

Larry led his friend out into the fresh air, hoping that it would clear both their heads. Teddy decided to write a story about primitive people who had a pet saber tooth. Flying reptiles would attack the people, and the cat would save their lives by heroically sacrificing itself.

#

Chapter Seven

Teddy sold three more stories over the course of a year, and he began reading the books in the store during his lunch breaks. In addition to the lurid fantasy magazines, he read the classics, from Homer's *Iliad* and Virgil's *Aeneid* to Faulkner, Hemingway and Virginia Woolf. He used the myths of the ancient world to plot his own tales, and he began doing research to get the facts right when he discussed science and technology in his writing. From time to time, the feminine voice told him more stories, but he also began to invent them on his own. Dr. Bell promoted him to assistant manager, and Candy finally agreed to marry him. The biggest problem that he faced was a growing phobia about talking to customers. He preferred to sit in the back room by himself, reading his books and typing his manuscripts. He had cleaned up the little back room with rags, hot water, bleach and patience. It almost felt like home, although it was barely bigger than a broom closet. Perhaps it had been a broom closet, before Dr. Bell squeezed the heavy walnut desk into it and made it his office.

Teddy nearly fell apart at the wedding, with almost two hundred people in attendance at the local Presbyterian church, but a bottle of unblended scotch whiskey, a gift from his father-in-law, fortified him just enough to get through the ceremony. He passed out that night or at least blacked out. He wished that he could remember his wedding night, but it was a total blank.   He kicked himself for failing to remember how his own wife looked naked.

Candy settled into domestic life easily enough, picking out furniture and appliances for the little starter home that her parents helped them buy. She seemed domestic enough, but she insisted that Teddy take her out dancing every Saturday night, as if they were still dating. She said that it would keep their romance alive. He thought it might kill him to be around so many people who were making so much noise and moving around so much, but he did it to keep his wife happy. He even caved in to her insistence that he write some serious literary fiction and submit it to the respectable magazines, like the *New Yorker* and *Atlantic Monthly*. He sent them his best stories, including the one about an elderly gentleman in a nursing home who believed that the doctors and nurses were aliens with plans to take over the Earth. His stories came back with form rejection letters, so he studied harder and tried harder to write serious literature, to please his wife with publication in a respectable genre. After all, he had worked very hard for a very long time to win her affection and her hand.

So he was totally shocked when a stunning brunette walked into the bookstore and he fell instantly and deeply in love with a woman he never had met before. She seemed familiar, but he was certain that he never had seen her before that amazing moment. As she strolled between the book shelves, he could hear a flute playing in his head, whistling a soft melody that stirred his heart and made him bold enough to walk up to her and introduce himself. He knew that it was wrong to feel this way, and even more wrong to act upon this feeling, but he felt bewitched by the very presence of such a beauty. When he heard her speak, he recognized the feminine voice which had guided him and told him stories. Fittingly, her name was Lorelei, the name of a mythical enchantress.

"May I help you find something?"

"I'm looking for art books," she said.

"Over here." He led her to the section with the big, heavy tomes filled with color photographs of paintings by the masters, ancient and modern.

"Oh, I didn't mean those. I mean books about how to draw and paint. I'm studying art at the university."

Teddy helped her to find some books in the back of the store, near the door to the back room where he wrote his stories, and he began talking about his dreams of becoming a famous author.

"That's very interesting," Lorelei said. "I'd love to be a famous artist, but most of us starve. Is it the same way for writers?"

"I'm afraid so. That's why I work here, to pay the bills."

"But don't you just love being around all these books? I mean, you're a writer, so books are your life, right?"

The flute music became louder and was joined by the tinkling of bells.

He knew better, knew that it was wrong, but he asked her out. Shyly gazing at her feet, she offered the excuse that she had exams to study for.

"Maybe some other time?"

"Sure." She left the store without buying anything.

Finding a copy of Boccaccio's *Decameron* among the art books, he pulled it off the shelf to put it with the medieval literature where it belonged, next to Chaucer's *Canterbury Tales*. The book slipped from his hand as *Plato's Dialogues* had done, and this time a young man wearing tights and an elaborately jeweled velvet tunic stood before him. The man had open sores all over his face.

"The plague is the punishment for our sins," he said.

"What sins?"

"We followed the foolish advice to eat, drink and be merry."

"And how did you catch the plague?" Teddy asked.

"The most venal of sins, fornication. First they said it was bad air, and then they said it was bad water, and then they drove out all the cats and rats from the city and burned the slums to the ground, but all their efforts were in vain. It was fornication, young man. Take my warning."

Before he could ask any more questions, the stranger melted to the floor and became a book again.

#

The alien slugs were anxious to accelerate the game, since the surgeons were preparing to remove the implant. They dared not risk exposure by abducting the subject from the hospital room, and another fever probably would not delay the surgery again, so they forgot all about completing their scientific study. Besides, they found the subject so entertaining that they wanted to get it all recorded, rent out a theatre and sell tickets to all the alien slugs on their home planet. They were sure to make a small fortune from this movie. Forgetting all about their lofty initial goal, they abandoned the experiment in order to make their fortunes with a low-budget horror movie. They had no way of knowing that a higher power had taken over the experiment and set an even loftier goal.

#

Father Diep took a leave of absence form his duties at the Church, needing to devote all of his time and energy to the guidance of his new disciple, all of his prayers and devotion to work toward bringing Robert Wells out of his coma. His dreams had become tinged with an element of conflict, no doubt the result of the Evil ones working against the liberation of the soul of humanity. His fingers played on the silver cross that hung on a silver chain around his neck. His black vestments were wrinkled from having been slept in, and he had omitted grooming for several days. His uncombed hair fell across his eyes as he read his Bible, squinting from eye strain. His voice grew raspy as he spoke aloud the words of Ecclesiastes, "Vanity! All is vanity!" He spent nearly every waking moment either in prayer or reading aloud from the Scriptures.

Always at the back of his mind was the sense of impending doom, accompanied by the light of hope. They were in such a close balance that he couldn't be certain which one would win. He felt driven to push the balance to the side of the light with all the force that he could muster. Surely God was on his side, and surely God wouldn't give him a burden that he couldn't bear. Yet sometimes he doubted his own strength, his own ability. Sometime he even doubted that God was listening, so he continued to pray and to read his Bible, as much to bolster his own faith as to instill it in his disciple.

#

Teddy read in a dusty old book from the bottom shelf in the myths and legends section of Bentley's Books that Lorelei appears in German legend as a young woman who committed suicide by throwing herself into the Rhine River when her lover spurned her. She was transformed into a siren, and she spends eternity sitting on a rock in the middle of the river, luring sailors to their deaths with a beautiful song that leads them to crash their boats on her rock in an attempt to get close to her. It was a fitting name, he thought, for his new love interest. He had no business feeling that way about any woman but his wife. Despite his intellectual and moral objections, however, he spent every day hoping that Lorelei would come back to the store, since he had no idea how to find her. In his spare moments he tried to picture her naked, lying on satin sheets with an inviting smile on her face, her pert breasts pointy with desire for him. Sometimes he could almost reach out and touch his vision of Lorelei, but then it would dissolve, unveiling the real world of work and home and city streets.

He heard flute music and tinkling bells every time he thought of her, and he felt warm inside whenever he pictured her standing among the bookshelves. He adored her small, thin body, almost ethereal, and every detail of her delicately carved face. Her meek and unassuming attitude testified that she was totally unaware of her stunning beauty, or at least that she did not place great value on it. He neglected his writing, and at home he was absent-minded, sitting in front of the television set that Candy's parents had given them for their first anniversary and barely noticing what program was on. Several times his wife found him staring at the test pattern late at night and had to lead him to bed.

"You work so hard," she said. "You must get more sleep." Helping him to undress, she hung his necktie on the rack and his coat on a hanger, laying out his slacks over the back of the bedroom chair the way he liked them, neat and orderly, each thing in its place. The shirt she tucked into the clothes hamper to be laundered with bleach, then pressed with plenty of starch. She knew her husband's penchant for neatness, which he often took to an unreasonable extreme. She was glad that his mother had given them an ironing board for a wedding present, even if it had been intended as an insult.

Candy was so concerned about his health that she allowed him to take her out to the movies on Saturday nights, instead of dancing, so it wouldn't tax his strength so much. Sitting in a darkened theatre and watching the show ought to renew his strength, not strain it.

She began working, minding other women's children and cleaning other women's houses, to pass the empty hours while Teddy was at work and to bring a little extra money into their household. Their meager budget, which always had been tight, was suffering from the rejection of Teddy's latest literary efforts. They had come to count on the extra money from his stories, and now it wasn't coming in any more. Apparently, Teddy's more serious efforts were not quite as marketable as his fantasies.

More worrisome than the shortage of funds to pay the milkman and then electric bill was her husband's inattentiveness toward her, which had come about suddenly, in a single day, after over a year of complete devotion to her and heroic attempts to fulfill all of her needs and desires. He no longer talked about having children, which had been his supreme dream when they first married. Although she searched for it, she found no evidence that he had been unfaithful to her. The only lipstick on his shirt collar was her own, the only perfume on his clothing her own scent or his aftershave. He gave her his pay check every Friday, and the modest allowance that she gave back to him was nowhere near enough to court another woman. And yet she had once heard him blurt out, when he had fallen asleep watching the television, a strange name: Lorelei.

#

Chapter Eight

The False Messengers searched the city for the alien spacecraft, coming every inch with their detectors, working in a grid pattern so as not to miss a single spot. They must locate, capture and sterilize these invaders. And they must locate the device that they had brought to the Earth. This most dangerous device could upset the delicate balance of power which kept the Messengers in control. Big men in black suits walked the streets, tuning the dials and pointing the antennae, tirelessly seeking out the device and the aliens who brought it. They haunted the spaces around shopping malls, office complexes, government buildings and liquor stores, the streets and alleys and parking lots. They finally settled upon a city park, a tiny square of grass and trees in the middle of downtown Berkeley, California, but they came too late. While the recovery teams were still driving up in their vans, the flying saucer took to the sky and disappeared into the vastness of interplanetary space.

Messenger Josiah pounded his fist on the desk. "The device is still here," he said. "I can sense it."

The others, the six minions who sat in his office, nodded in agreement, even though they certainly lacked the refinement of perception which would allow them to sense the presence of the device.

"We will locate it," one of the minions said.

"You will retrieve it," Messenger Josiah commanded.

#

When Teddy arrived home on Friday afternoon, wistfully daydreaming about Lorelei, instead of a little stucco house he found himself standing in front of a stone temple with statues of grotesque gargoyles standing on either side of the entrance, a double door made of iron that refused to open when he pushed and pulled on it. This turn of events did not surprise him, since he had found that some sort of punishment was always imposed upon him whenever he made an unethical choice. There was the battlefield in Korea, and there was the iron prison in Rome, and he even had a dim memory of gazing into the pit of Hell. Yet he could not help believing that he was meant to be with Lorelei, and that his real mistake had been marrying Candy. Standing helplessly outside the locked fortress that was his home, he silently prayed for the feminine voice to guide him, to rescue him from his own foolishness. Instead, a large man with coffee-and-cream skin appeared and spoke to him in a low, deep voice.

"This is the gate of nature," the big man said. "You may not enter."

"Then what should I do?"

"Find the gate where you may enter." The man folded his arms and disappeared in a mist.

Teddy walked down the sidewalk, avoiding stepping on the cracks as he had done when he was very young, thinking that maybe he was on the wrong block, looking for the familiar sight of his orange stucco house with the red brick front porch and white aluminum awnings. Here and there people had parked cars out on the street, and he wished that he had a car so he could find his way home faster and without getting so tired from walking. If he wanted to buy a car, he would have to earn the money for it himself. His wife's parents felt that their generosity had been quite overextended with the down payment on their house, and his own mother had attended the ceremony only as a matter of form, giving them an ironing board as a wedding gift and totally ignoring their first anniversary. Near the middle of the next block, he found a temple with a statue of a goddess standing on the right-hand side of the entrance, a double door made of oak that refused to open when he pushed and pulled on it.

The feminine voice spoke to him now, the voice of Lorelei saying, "You may not enter the gate of reason, since you are behaving in a quite unreasonable manner."

"What is that supposed to mean?" he asked out loud, but he received no answer.

Walking down another block, he wondered what he would find next. With a sigh of relief, he spotted his own house. He approached the door with some trepidation, but it opened easily and he entered his own living room. "Candy, I'm home!" he called out.

No answer. Candy was not at home. He sat down on the sofa and wondered where she could be at this late hour. The street lights were coming on outside, and most of the neighbors must be sitting down for dinner.

The feminine voice said, "You have to put your slippers on to walk toward the dawn."

"What is that supposed to mean?"

"You have entered the gates of wisdom, and now you must pass through the Ordeal."

"Why?"

"It is the only way to find your true love."

"What if I refuse?"

"That is entirely your choice."

Teddy considered that choice, which was undoubtedly another test. He would rather not go through another ordeal, but on the other hand, he longed to find his true love. He knew that he had made a big mistake with Candy, who was more of a challenge to be conquered than a woman to be loved and cherished. He hoped and prayed that his true love would turn out to be Lorelei, that he could have his marriage annulled and spend the rest of his life with his true soul mate.

"Okay," he said, thinking, *This can't be nearly as hard as the algebra test.*

The big dark-skinned man from the first temple appeared and led him outside. "You understand," he said, "that you can change your mind at any junction, any turning point in the series of Ordeals."

"Series? You mean there's more than one?"

"Yes, there are twelve in all. They are difficult and dangerous, but you will not be alone."

The large man led him down the sidewalk until they saw another man walking toward him. "Ah, the high priest of Zoroaster approaches. I leave you to his care." He vanished , leaving Teddy alone to meet the ominous-looking, black-robed figure who was walking toward him.

He stood still, watching the third man approach, and presently he made out the form of Dr. Bell. Relieved, he ran up to his boss and begged him to explain what was going on.

"You will face twelve trials," the old man told him, "twelve tests of your courage and moral principles. A friend will accompany you, and he will also face the same tests. If you do well, you will find true love." He looked perfectly comfortable and proper in his long black priest's robes, and he sounded completely natural mouthing those strange words.

"And if I fail?"

"You will succeed. I have faith in you."

#

Zoroaster, also known as Zarathustra, was a prophet in ancient Iran who founded a religion that competed with Judaism. Many early Christians accepted what came to be known as the Zoroastrian heresy. The Zoroastrian scriptures, the *Avesta*, describe the universe as a struggle between personified Truth and Lies. The role of humanity is to sustain Truth by doing good works.

#

On Saturday afternoon, Angelica and her mother sat together in Robert Wells' hospital room, watching him lie there doing nothing, neither waking nor sleeping, but staring at the ceiling. The doctors had scheduled surgery for Monday morning, declaring their husband and father to be fit enough to survive the excision of the brain tumor. Edna read aloud from the entertainment columns in the *Chronicle*, and Angelica talked about her internship with a local veterinarian. She had assisted in the birth of a show horse on her first day.

"He was coming out breach, so we had to push him back in and turn him around. It was the most amazing experience, to watch the foal taking his first few breaths and standing up on those wobbly legs!"

She thought that she might have seen the hint of a smile on her father's lips, but she couldn't be sure.

"Your symphony is a great success," Edna said. "Now the London Symphony wants to buy the rights. It's going to spread around the world, and you're going to be a respected composer. Already, several universities want to pay you to speak to their students. As soon as you're well, that is."

They continued talking to him, mother and daughter, encouraging him to be strong and brave, to come through the surgery and come home to them. Edna felt the beginnings of a deeper love than the flowering of romance that had led her to marry him when they were young and passionate. She came to the realization that she loved him for the depth of his soul, not for his money or the things that he bought for her. She also formed a stronger bond with her daughter than she ever had thought possible, concluding that a real tragedy was bringing out the best in all of them. She hoped and prayed that her husband would come through the operation alive and well, with no brain damage.

Through the window the women could see a pair of robins flitting around, picking up twigs from the ground and carrying them up to a tree branch where they were building a nest. They considered that a good sign.

#

Teddy and the big man walked together until they came to a stone pyramid with signs of weathering from great age, a totally incongruous structure in the setting of Berkeley, California. Standing near the entrance and waving to him, was Teddy's friend Bobby, now possessing both legs, as if he never had gone to Korea and lost a limb. The two young men ran to each other and embraced, laughing and jumping up and down.

"I'm so glad to see you," Teddy said.

"Me, too. I could never do this alone."

"Me, neither."

"I've already been very nearly been crushed to death by a python, so I'm not looking forward to whatever else they have in store for us," Bobby explained.

"Why did you agree to do it?"

"Ah, love!"

"Ah."

"You see, I saw the most beautiful woman, and she was about to kill herself because a man was forcing himself on her, and she was only saved at the last possible moment by our priest here."

Dr. Bell, still dressed in the black robes of a priest, began to pray out loud. They listened carefully, but the old man was speaking a strange language that neither of them had ever heard before. He swung a brass censer from a long chain, filling the air with the dense aroma of frankincense. Then he dipped his fingers into a small bowl of holy water and made signs in the air and on their foreheads. Finally, the ceremony completed, he said in English, "Before you may enter the Temple of the Ordeal, you must first prove yourselves worthy. You will be tempted by three women, and you must neither touch them nor speak to them."

He led them to a palm tree in the courtyard of the Temple of the Ordeal and told them to sit down and wait.

Suddenly, a bear crashed through the bushes and charged straight toward them. Teddy started to get up to run away, but Bobby tugged at his sleeve, pulled out a flute from under his coat, and began playing a lighthearted tune. The bear stopped in a cloud of dust, swayed from side to side, then turned and lumbered away, as if it never had threatened them or even seen them.

It wasn't long before three women in exotic eastern costumes came to tempt them. They danced around the two young men, jiggling their hips and showing off their bare bellies. They made music with bells that hung from satin cords around their ankles, and Teddy suddenly realized that the leather strap with sleigh bells was once again hanging over his shoulders. Bobby pulled out his flute again and began to play the most beautiful melody that Teddy had ever heard. The two remained silent and made no move to touch the women, even though they were quite beautiful. Teddy wanted no other woman but Lorelei, and Bobby seemed to be under the spell of a similar enchantress. Bored with the women's futile entreaties for them to come and join them in love's embrace, he began shaking the strap with the bells, and the tinkling sound made the women dance in circles, seemingly oblivious to the two young men. *So*, he thought, *Bobby's flute is not the only magical musical instrument here. There are also my bells.*

After several minutes, a loud thunderclap frightened the women away. The large man appeared and led the two young men into the temple and down a long corridor with a gabled stone ceiling.. They emerged into a garden that was somehow magically bathed in sunlight, even though it must be covered by the stone ceiling of the pyramid that housed it.

The big man said, "You must once again refrain from speaking to the women, no matter what happens." And then he left them.

"The same test again," Teddy remarked.

"Where did you get those bells?" Bobby asked.

"Where'd you get that flute?"

Neither of them knew the answer to either question.

They wandered in the shade of tropical palms, ferns and banana trees, their feet cushioned by a luxurious carpet of grass. Sprinkled all over the jungle floor were orchids and bromeliads with blooms in a shocking array of bright colors. Vines curled around the tree trunks and sprouted flowers of their own, all brightly colored like the rainbow, only more intense.

Bobby said, "I hear running water. Let's find it."

Being thirsty, Teddy agreed.

When they had walked another hundred yards, they found a marble fountain in the shape of a fish, and under the shade of a giant fern next to the fountain, Lorelei lay sleeping. As they approached, she began to stir. They stopped a few feet away from the beautiful woman and waited for her to wake up.

When she saw them, she cried out with joy, "Bobby and Teddy! It's so good to see you. Where are we? What are we doing in this place?"

Teddy opened his mouth to answer, but Bobby clamped a hand over his mouth and knocked him to the ground, pinning him down with a wrestling hold.

"What are you doing?" Lorelei demanded. "Why won't you speak to me?"

Bobby kept his jaws clamped shut and his hand firmly over Teddy's mouth.

"Stop fighting, you two!"

Bobby refused to release his hold on Teddy, no matter how hard he struggled to break free.

Lorelei began to weep, and then she ran away.

"He told us not to speak," Bobby said, letting go of his friend.

"But we hurt her feelings," Teddy protested.

"This is all an illusion. It's only in your mind."

The words sounded familiar, like something from a nightmare.

"I mean to pass these tests and win Lorelei, and I am not going to let you mess it up for me."

"Lorelei?" Teddy asked. "I thought she was for me."

"You're already married. How do you expect to pass a test of your moral principles, if your goal is to cheat on your wife? And make a whore out of Lorelei!"

"Then you should have let me talk to her, since I'm going to fail the test anyway."

While they were still arguing about whether they should have answered Lorelei's questions, an ugly old woman approached them. "Where have you been my husband?" she asked, pointing a gnarled finger directly at Teddy.

Teddy, still under the command not to speak to women, shook his head no and thought, *That is not my wife.*

"Things are not as they appear." She instantly transformed into the figure of Candy in her chiffon dress, the one she had worn that Saturday afternoon when Teddy had shown her his first check for his first published story. Even now, with Lorelei on his mind, his heart beat faster at the sight of his beautiful wife. He reached out to her with one hand, but at that moment a streak of lightning flashed up from the ground between them and she ran away in terror.

No one appeared to advise them, and Teddy failed to hear any advice from the feminine voice in his head, so they wandered through the garden again, wondering what the next ordeal would be. Teddy began brushing off his jacket with his hands, knocking feathers off of it and wondering where they had come from. His arms began to itch intolerably, so he scratched at his sleeves and knocked off more feathers. After several minutes of futile attempts to rid himself of the feathers, he came to the conclusion that they were growing on his skin, that they were part of him. "Well," he said, "I certainly do hope that things are not as they appear." He laughed a little, more out of despair than from amusement.

"Why, you're covered with feathers! You're turning into a bird! Exactly like a giant owl. I hope nothing like that happens to me."

In the next clearing, they saw Lorelei again, a vision of beauty with her long, silky dark hair and exquisitely sparkling eyes, about to hang herself by leaping from a tree with a rope tied to the branch at one end and around her neck with the other. Teddy clapped his hands, technically not speaking to her, but she didn't hear him or didn't pay them any attention. Bobby frantically pulled out his flute and played a delightful melody, but it had no effect on her. Teddy's bells jingled while they ran to get closer to her, but Lorelei paid no attention and continued tightening the knots in her rope.

Dr. Bell suddenly appeared in front of them, held up his hand and commanded, "Stop!" Turning around to face Lorelei, he issued the same command to her. Lorelei sat down on the tree branch and, looking dazed and confused, loosened the loop of rope around her neck and pulled it off over her head.

Dr. Bell stood under the tree and held out his hands to her.

"How did I get here?" she asked, climbing down with the priest's assistance.

"That is no matter. You must come with me." Bentley and Lorelei began walking away from the tree and toward the river.

Bobby and Teddy started to follow the pair, but Bentley turned to them and said, "You cannot be with your true love yet. You have not earned the privilege." Waving his hand in the air, he produced a mist that enveloped him and Lorelei, and they disappeared.

"Where should we go next?" Teddy asked. "Any idea what the next test will be?"

Before Bobby could answer, a gigantic wild boar charged at them, knocking down the ferns and other plants in its path. Teddy was sure that they were going to die, since neither of them had any weapons, but Bobby calmly pulled his flute out from under his jacket and began to play. The boar, seemingly enchanted by the music, stopped in its track and began swaying from side to side in a sort of dance.

"Will you quit panicking? You already saw how I tamed the bear."

"Sorry, I guess I'm a slow learner."

"Come on," Bobby said. "Let's get out of here before the spell wears off."

They found a path and followed it through the foliage until three boys blocked their path, shouting insults and throwing rocks at them. "Sissy boys!" they yelled. "You couldn't frighten a butterfly!"

Ducking under the shower of rocks and crossing his arms over his face, Teddy heard his bells tinkling. Picking up a rock from the ground to toss it back at the boys, he noticed that the boys had begun to dance. He stood still, and the bells quit tinkling, and the boys immediately stopped dancing and began throwing rocks again. Testing a theory, Teddy jiggled the leather strap and made the bells sound again. The boys immediately stopped throwing rocks and began dancing again, just as the women had done when he absent-mindedly played with his bells.

"Let's go," he said, and he and Bobby put some distance between themselves and the naughty boys, keeping the bells tinkling until they were well out of sight.

They continued walking aimlessly until two priests appeared and led them to a table set with fine china plates already filled with food, plus crystal glassware, sterling silver place settings and a sumptuous feast of roasted meats, fruits and vegetables, bread and cheeses laid out in serving bowls that appeared to be made out of rainbows. They sat down and filled their goblets with wine that tasted sweet and boasted a fruity aroma. Bobby took a bite of the food on his plate and declared it divine. Teddy, who rarely ate more than a soda cracker, found himself voraciously devouring the food, from the fresh fruit and sweet rolls to the beef roast, sweet potatoes and mixed vegetables. His appetite seemed to have no end.

The priests stood by, chanting in some foreign tongue that they could not understand.

"Come on," Bobby said. "We have to go now and take the next test."

"In a minute," Teddy mumbled while still chewing his food.

"We have to go," he insisted. "We didn't come here to fill our bellies."

Teddy might never have left the table, but a lion came charging through the garden, heading straight toward them with a hungry look on his face. Bobby was already tugging at his feathery sleeve, and he got up and ran beside his friend to escape the ravenous beast.

"Play your flute!" Teddy shouted.

"No!"

Teddy thought that they might end up in the lion's belly, but a clap of thunder knocked them off their feet and frightened the lion away.

"Why didn't you play your flute?"

"What, and let you go back to the table? Don't you know that it was another test? You must overcome the desire to fill your belly in order to fill your heart and your mind."

"Oh. I really am a slow learner."

"No kidding."

Dr. Bell appeared in his priest's robes and shook his head. "You have failed," he announced, "and so early in the Ordeal."

#

Chapter Nine

Early Monday morning, the nurses ushered Candy and Angelica out of the room and prepared Robert Wells for his surgery. They shaved his head and painted it with iodine, and they inserted a new IV into his left arm for the anesthesiologist to use. Then the orderlies came in and moved his limp body onto a gurney, which they rolled into the operating theatre. The surgeons studied the MRI and conventional X-rays, planning where to drill and saw through the skull for the best angle of attack on the tumor. They hoped to get the whole thing out, and they thought that it should be relatively simple. The whole thing was less than a three inches in circumference. The real problem would be the thin strands of tissue radiating from the tumor, extending into deeper parts of the patient's brain.

It was entirely possible that they could tug on those threads and pull them out, rather than resorting to the hazardous process of digging though good brain tissue to get to them. They had already discussed the possibility that they might have to leave them *in situ*, rather than risk severe damage to the brain. In any case, the removal of the main body of the tumor would relieve the pressure on the brain which was keeping the patient in a coma. The grueling procedure would be almost as hard on the doctors as on the patient, but they felt confident of a positive outcome.

#

The two young men felt crushed, as if a hammer had fallen onto their heads and knocked them senseless. How could they have failed? They didn't speak to the women, and they didn't even speak to Lorelei, even though they had been severely tempted.

"We didn't say a word," Teddy protested.

Dr. Bell pointed straight at Teddy in the same way that the old woman had pointed to him, and said, "You would have spoken, if your friend had not stopped you. And you never would have left the table without his urging. He has earned the right to go on to the next Ordeal, but you must stop here." He reached out his right hand, and the old woman appeared out of thin air. "This is your wife. Will you take her?"

Teddy spoke without thinking and without regret. "Yes, I will." He figured that he deserved to be married to a hag, as punishment for his sins.

The old woman instantly transformed into Candy, but this time she was covered in feathers as if she were Teddy's twin. The priest took her by the hand and led her away, leaving the two young men alone again.

Teddy heard the feminine voice inside his head again, the voice of Lorelei saying, "I can't rescue you from the world of your own mind. You will have to save yourself." Teddy took this to mean that he had shirked responsibility for his own fate, always praying for others to get him out of trouble.

"I don't want to do this alone," Bobby said. "Will you come with me?"

"Yes," Teddy said without hesitation. If he must accept Candy as his wife, then he was willing to help his friend to win Lorelei. He felt a great sense of relief that Candy was not an old hag, after all.

The two young men walked toward the entrance to a stone building, but after Bobby went through the doorway, Teddy found his feet stuck to the ground.

"You may not enter," Dr. Bell said. "Don't worry about your friend. He will succeed. In fact, he has already succeeded. Look." He pointed up to the sky, and following the old man's arm with his gaze, Teddy saw Bobby and Lorelei sitting on a cumulus cloud, embracing and kissing.

"Here is your bride," Bentley the priest said, and Candy appeared again. She was still covered in feathers.

"Why, you look just like an owl!" she cried out. "You have great big eyes and soft, fluffy wings."

"So do you," he said, opening his arms wide.

They embraced and hugged and talked about their feathers,.

"Your belly is so soft!" she exclaimed.

"Yours, too. Hey, quit tickling me!"

Dr. Bell cleared his throat, and they looked at him, still embracing. Now you may enter the Temple of Nature," he said. He waved his hand, and a double iron door appeared in front of them. It opened easily to their touch, and beyond the threshold they saw a delightful forest filled with incense cedars, oak trees and berry bushes.

Teddy walked into the woods arm in arm with Candy, wondering whether she would give birth to children or lay eggs. The trees looked oddly gray, compared to the bright colors of the jungle which they had left behind. In fact, they wondered whether they had become color blind upon entering the Temple of Nature.

Their troubles seemed to be over, except for the itchy feathers, when suddenly they heard the sound of a chain saw. Somebody was cutting down the forest, and as an owl, he lived in a tree. One by one, the trees crashed down to the ground, bouncing several times until their branches snapped under the weight of their trunks.

"Come on!" he shouted, running away from a falling cedar and dragging Candy along with him. They had gone about a hundred yards when he had to stop and catch his breath.

"Can't we fly?" she asked.

"I don't know."

"Well, let's try it. We're birds, after all."

Having nothing to lose, Teddy leaped into the air and spread his wings. He fell to the ground in an awkward belly flop, getting a beak full of dirt for his effort. He rolled over and commented, "I guess we're too heavy to fly. It was a good idea, anyway."

A sultry silence fell over the woods, and they realized that the chain saw had stopped. Now it was raining, or more accurately water was falling from the branches of tall pines, cedars and oak trees. Hot, heavy drops of water splattered on the ground and on their feathers. The air smelled salty, as if they were near the ocean.

"Do you think we'll be like this forever?" Candy asked.

"Like what?"

"You know, feathered." She shook her shoulders, sending a cascade off water off her feathers onto the ground.

Teddy shook his own feathers, and the water rolled off of him. "We're waterproof! Cool!"

"Yes, but will we always be owls?"

"No idea. But I do hope that we stay together forever."

"Aw, that's so sweet!"

"Whatever happened to us? I mean, we used to be so much in love."

"We still are, silly. It's just that the passion has cooled, now that we're older. More mature. At least I am. Don't you feel more grown up than you did a couple years ago? Before you settled down?"

"I feel different. But it's like I let you down, took you for granted."

"You were working so hard, trying to make a good life for us. But now we don't need any money, just a cozy nest in one of these trees.

"I sure hope that guy with the chain saw doesn't come back."

"Me, too."

#

Owls are carnivorous, but they will resort to eating acorns, nuts and berries when no meat is available. Their favorite foods are small rodents, which they usually swallow whole. The gizzard, a part of the owl's stomach, bundles up the indigestible parts -- the bones, fur, claws and teeth -- into a pellet that the owl regurgitates and spits out. Larger owls will hunt rabbits, foxes and birds as large as ducks, while smaller species hunt mice, shrews and voles. Their diet also includes insects, spiders, earthworms, snails and crabs.

#

The surgeons began the delicate process of excising the tumor from Robert Wells' brain, pulling back the flaps of skin and pinning them out of the way, probing the tissue and clamping off the tiny capillaries that fed the offending mass of foreign tissue. Nurses dabbed the area with gauze swatches and cotton balls, soaking off the blood so the surgeons could see the tumor. It looked like nothing they ever had seen before, and they had removed many cancers from many patients. This tumor looked like an alien creature from a low-budget science fiction movie. Nearly two centimeters in diameter and barely as thick as a washrag, shaped roughly like a manta ray, it was a rubbery mass of gray endothelial tissue bathed in mucous, lying across the back of the patient's brain. In short, it was a gut, which they feared might have begun digesting the patient's brain. One of the nurse assistants actually fainted at the sight of it, and the surgical nurses had seen plenty of gore in their careers. This thing had the appearance of a parasite, although they could not imagine how such a thing could have gotten inside the patient's skull.

The alien slugs chose not to intervene, since the implant's batteries were nearly dead, anyway. Besides, invading a hospital would mean risking exposure to witnesses and possibly security cameras; they dared not betray their presence on this alien planet. They shut down the experiment and prepared to return to their home planet with a cinema verité production that would make their fortunes.

The surgeons proceeded with the operation, cutting off the blood supply to the mass of tumor and tugging gently. To their relief, the tendrils which had extended into the patient's brain came out with the main mass, so they did not have to dig for them or leave them in. After six hours, they declared it a success and called in another surgeon, one who was not exhausted, to close up.

When Robert Wells lay in the recovery room, his wife and daughter came in to watch him and wait for him to wake up. His head was wrapped up in bloody gauze, and his complexion was gray with yellow streaks from the ordeal. They watched and waited, but their husband and father did not wake up. After several hours, a nurse assured them that he was now sleeping normally and not in a coma, but it looked the same to them. He was transferred to intensive care, where they could visit any time and not only during visiting hours, but the nurse advised them to go home and get some sleep. Robert Wells was expected to sleep a full eight hours or more before waking up.

#

Teddy sat down under an oak tree and watched for rodents. He had an insatiable appetite for mouse flesh, something he never had experienced before. The idea of swallowing a furry little creature whole, digesting its raw flesh and then coughing up a pellet filled with the indigestible parts, the fur and the bones, seemed like the most satisfying activity in the world. Candy managed to climb up to the lowest branches of the oak, using the claws on her feet, and she was arranging twigs and leaves into a cozy nest in a fork between two branches.

Suddenly, a rolling ball of fur plopped to the ground and scuttled away. It was a raccoon, suddenly displaced from its nest by a persistent female owl.

Teddy folded his wings behind his head, feeling that everything was right with the world. The man with the chain saw did not come back. The cool night air soothed his itches, and everything was right. He did wish that he could fly; it would make it so much easier to catch rabbits and field mice.

Suddenly, he was blind! A searing pain hit him on the back of his head, and he couldn't see a thing. "What's happening?" he screamed.

"It's only the sun," Candy said. "We're nocturnal creatures now, so come on up here and sleep in our nest until night time."

"I'm blind!"

"You're an owl in daylight. Of course you're blind."

"Why does it hurt so much?"

"I don't know. I don't feel any pain."

"It's like something hit me on the back of my head." Slowly his vision began to clear and he could make out a few of the objects around him, but they were dim shapes without detail and he still felt that he was nearly blind.

A soft breeze settled softly upon their shoulders as they dozed off, slumbering to the music of humming insects that hovered around the flowers in the underbrush.

The implant was gone, but he continued his other life in the dream world. Without input from the implant or the amusement park's computer, his own mind continuously created the world for him while he slept in the hospital bed. He still did not remember his life as Robert Wells, his mansion, his wife and daughter, or his other woman in the condominium apartment, or his career composing movie music.

In fact, he barely remembered his life as a store clerk and a writer of fantasy fiction, now that he had become an owl. He didn't mind that loss, since he found himself living in the beautiful world of nature, free from the stresses of civilized society, the clocks, the traffic, the gates and fences, the need to collect numbers on slips of paper and hand over those numbers in exchange for the necessities of life. Here he could obtain food and shelter directly, without the intermediary of dollars and coins.

#

Edna arrived home exhausted, but she had trouble falling asleep due to an intolerable itching that began on her back and spread across her shoulders onto her arms. She slept fitfully, dreaming that she was sitting in a tree, as she had done when she was a child. She used to love climbing up the old fig tree on the edge of her parents' vineyard, where they grew some of the finest cabernet grapes in the state, perhaps in the world. California wines might not have the cachet of imported vintages, but a five-dollar bottle of California wine tasted ten times better than a twenty-dollar bottle from France. Imported wines had their prices highly inflated to cover the shipping costs.

Besides, her parents maintained their fortune by growing and crushing the grapes, fermenting them and bottling fine wines. Technically, their employees did all the work, but the family managed the business and her brothers inspected the vines on horseback every day until they went off to college. Perhaps that was why she had chosen this mansion, since it had the most verdant gardens she could ever hope for. It even had grape vines climbing trellises in a dozen different spots. They were only table grapes, not wine grapes, but they did help to make her feel at home.

In her dreams she was building a nest for herself and her husband, who looked like a big fat owl. The dreams came back to her the next day when she visited Rob in the hospital, and he was talking in his sleep. Talking was not exactly the right word for it, since he was hooting like an owl.

"Is he ever going to wake up?" she asked the doctor.

"Every case is unique," he said. "Brain surgery is a great shock to the system, and the patient needs time to heal."

"How much time?"

"It's hard to tell. Some patients wake in a day, while others stay unconscious for as long as a week. It's nothing to worry about."

She fretted about it all day, but there was nothing she could do.

#

As the shades of twilight settled softly over the woods, Candy and Teddy woke up from their daylong sleep and climbed down from their tree.

"I'm hungry," she said.

"Me too."

Just then, Teddy saw a fat, juicy beetle crossing the path a few feet ahead. He hopped up, flapping his nearly useless wings, and stomped on it with his claws, then dealt it a death blow with his sharp beak and gobbled it up.

"Hey! You could have saved some for me!" Candy put her wingtips on her hips to emphasize her displeasure with his greedy behavior.

"Sorry. You can have the next one. I promise."

Candy stopped at a berry bush and began gobbling up the little purple fruits. "Not too bad," she said. "Try some."

Teddy plucked a green berry with his sharp beak, detected a nasty bitter taste and then spat it out.

"The red ones," she said. "Eat the ripe ones."

He ate a few berries, but they were nowhere near as tasty as the beetle. Still, his empty stomach demanded more food, and little else seemed available.

"There's one!" He pointed with his wingtip at another beetle that had wandered into the path.

She hopped onto the insect and dispatched it with a style and grace that he admired, the finesse that she had always shown on the dance floor. Teddy then realized that he had failed to fully appreciate her finest qualities. All that he had seen were her blonde hair and blue eyes, not the person that she truly was.

Suddenly, they heard some kind of huge beast crashing through the underbrush. Frightened, they ran off into the thick bushes and hid from whatever was threatening them. .

#

Chapter Ten

Edna and Angelica sat by Rob Wells' bedside, feeling desperate to wake him up. His surgery on Monday had been declared successful, but now on Saturday he was still sleeping. The women did not like to use the word "coma", since it had such negative connotations, but they wondered how this could be anything else, since normal sleep shouldn't last more than eight or ten hours.

Since they had moved him out of intensive care, the regular visiting hours applied again, so they had to arrange their schedules to make time to see their husband and father. He looked more like himself, now that the swelling had gone down and the nurses had replaced the bulky wrappings with a pad of gauze taped over the back of his head, where the surgeons had cut him open. The private room was costing a small fortune, even though his health insurance covered almost half of it. Edna made a mental note to switch their policy to another company with better coverage.

"I brought you something," Edna said, pulling a small tape recorder out of her purse. "I recorded a performance of your Symphony of the Birds. It's better when you hear it in person, but since that isn't possible . . . " Her voice trailed off, and she pushed the Play button.

Flutes and piccolos chirped out the major theme, while the cello and timpani backed them up. Clarinets picked up the theme, and then the strings joined in. The music sounded like birds singing, at least to human ears, but not to owl ears.

When the recording had finished, Angelica said, "Everybody is trying to help you, Dad, but you have to wake up. You have to do it, yourself. We can't do it for you."

#

Teddy and Candy were trembling with fear as the sound of a huge beast crashing through the bushes assaulted their sensitive owl ears. Owls have directional hearing which helps them to locate prey, so they knew exactly where to look when the big dark man emerged into the clearing where they had been eating berries and bugs.

"Where are you, my little friends?"

They shuffled their feet and timidly began walking toward him. They felt that they had lost control of their own feet, since they wanted to run away, but they were moving toward the big man.

"There you are!" he said, picking up both of them in his massive arms. He chuckled and hugged them and set them down on the soft ground.

The owls began straightening out their feathers, which had become ruffled in his grip.

"How would you two like to enter the Temple of Wisdom? Owls are supposed to be wise, you know."

"I don't know," Candy said hesitantly. "I kind of like it here."

"Well," Teddy offered, "it is kind of boring, except when that guy with the chain saw was here. He isn't going to come back, is he?"

"Oh, him," the big dark man said. "Don't you worry about Foster. He was only clearing out some of the dead trees, for fire safety."

Just then it occurred to Candy that they did not know the big man's name, so she asked him.

"Monostatos, but you can call me Stat, for short." He led the two owls through the woods and out into the streets of Berkeley.

"It's very dark out here," Candy said.

"Aren't we supposed to have good night vision?" Teddy asked.

Stat emitted a huge belly laugh. "Look at yourselves. You aren't owls any more."

Teddy looked at Candy, then stretched out his arms and inspected them. The feathers were all gone, and once again he was wearing the sport coat and slacks that he wore to work in his job at the -- he couldn't remember where he worked, but at least he did remember that he was a human and not a bird.

"Follow me," Stat said, and he set off down the block toward the Temple of Wisdom, a stone monument with oak doors that stood open as if to welcome them.

They followed him inside and found themselves at the foot of a terraced mountain. Stat climbed up easily, and soon he was standing at the first level, waiting for his little friends to catch up. They gasped for breath, bending down to grab at bushes to drag themselves upward, and when they finally reached the flat ground, they fell down exhausted. They could hear distant, beautiful music from an instrument that they thought must be a harp.

"Is that the heavenly music of the spheres?" Teddy asked.

"Could be," Stat said.

Candy observed, "It's divine."

People began walking past them, men and women who carried heavy stones on their backs and could not stand up straight because of the weight.

"Why are they carrying rocks?" Candy asked. "Are they building something? Or clearing a field for planting?"

"Pride," Stat said. "They stood tall and proud in life, so now they must learn to be humble. Come on, let's go to the next terrace."

Teddy found his breathing labored and his feet heavy. The only thing that kept him going was the hope that, if he climbed high enough, he might find Lorelei. She would reach down from the clouds and lift him up into Heaven, rescuing him from the drudgery of his life.

Stat turned back and looked into Teddy's eyes. "You're backsliding," he said. "That's why it's so hard for you to climb."

"Can you read my thoughts?"

"Sometimes."

The climb became easier as they grew used to the altitude, but still it taxed their strength and made their breathing heavy. On the next higher level they found people wandering around with their eyes sewn shut, all of them wearing drab brown robes that reached past their feet and blended into the soil upon which they walked.

"Envy," Stat said. "They are being taught to refrain from desiring what others possess."

Night began to fall, and the big man produced a big blanket from under his robes. For the first time, Teddy noticed how beautiful Stat's robes looked, White robes with purple trim that never looked soiled, not even when he sat in the dirt. The blanket was a patchwork quilt with images of flowers, animals and people embroidered on the squares.

"We are not allowed to travel at night," he said, "so let's get some sleep."

Teddy and Candy fell asleep in each other's arms, covered by Stat's huge blanket, while the penitents continued wandering around with their eyes sewn shut, as blind as the owl in daylight.

#

Dante divided his Purgatory into seven terraces, one for each of the seven deadly sins. Sinful souls who repented might enter Purgatory instead of being punished in the Inferno, but only a few might rise up into Heaven after doing penance in Purgatory. Only completely purified souls were allowed to approach God in Heaven.

#

Edna was facing a crisis. With the huge medical bills and without Rob's income, she was finding it impossible to make ends meet. Rather than dip into her meager savings right away, she sent her husband's new Mercedes back to the dealer, finding it unnecessary as well as impossible to make the payments and keep up the insurance. She had to let most of the servants go, keeping only the butler and the gardener. She had asked them all whether a raccoon had gotten into the garden or the house, but none of them had seen it. Yet Edna kept seeing it, nearly every day.

For the first time in her life, she was cleaning her own house and cooking her own meals. Cooking wasn't exactly the right word for it, since she was getting by on cold sandwiches, fresh fruit and tossed salads. She was terribly afraid of burning down the kitchen if she tried using the stove, but she had managed to figure out how to work the coffee maker.

She stayed up late at night, fearing the strange dreams that had suddenly intruded into her slumber. In some dreams she was a plain middle class housewife working as a servant for other, more prosperous women. In the real nightmares, she was running for her life with wild beasts chasing after her, or slogging through the pits of Hell and witnessing the punishment of damned souls. She found it so upsetting that she had begun smoking cigarettes again, a nasty habit which she had given up when she graduated from college more than twenty years ago.

Edna began earning pocket money by writing articles for the local newspaper, starting with a historical piece about her family's vineyard. The liberal arts education that her parents had provided for her didn't qualify her for many jobs. She wished that they had sent her to business school with her brothers, who would inherit most of the family fortune and who now ran the family business. Mom and Dad held traditional values, so they expected her to marry well and live off her husband. She dared not ask them for money now, but she dialed the telephone anyway. At least she could tell her troubles to Mom and get some sympathy.

"Your father and I warned you not to marry beneath your station," Mom said. "You could have had half a dozen suitable husbands, but you chose to tie the knot with that working man. You made your own bed, darling, and now you must lie in it."

The clichés didn't make Mom's criticism any lighter. Edna decided to bite the bullet and put her jewelry up for auction. Why, the diamond necklace alone could get her through one more month.

#

The three travelers in the Temple of Wisdom woke up to the pleasant sound of birds singing, but they were still surrounded by the blind penitents. Stat folded up his blanket and led them upward to the third level. Here they found themselves lost in a shroud of acrid smoke with lost souls striving to find their way out. Teddy and Candy coughed and choked on the acrid atmosphere.

"Wrath," Stat said. "Their burning fury has blinded them. Let's go up to the fourth level, before you two choke to death."

Teddy wondered why Stat didn't seem to be bothered by the bad air, and why he never got tired or breathed heavily while they were climbing.

As if he had read Teddy's mind, Stat said, "I am not made of flesh and blood, but of dreams and gossamer."

They ascended again, following Stat, coughing and choking in the smoky air, until they emerged from the smoke onto another flat level. Here they found people running around the terrace, never stopping or even slowing down.

"Sloth," Stat said. "They were lazy in life, so now they must become dynamic." Looking down at

Teddy, he said, "That never was your problem, was it?"

"No," Candy said. "Teddy is the most hard-working man I know."

Blushing, Teddy looked down at the ground. He didn't want to admit to Candy that he had stayed out late trying to find another woman. She must never know about Lorelei, and why should she, since the affair never was consummated. It had been a mere fantasy, and at this moment he loved the reality of Candy infinitely more than the illusion of Lorelei. "I meant you, silly. Let's get out of here before it gets dark again," he said. "We couldn't possibly sleep with all these people running around."

The air had grown quite thin as they climbed higher, but they found it easier to breathe the more purified atmosphere, compared to the thicker but less refined air below. On the fifth level, they found people lying face down on the ground, trying but failing to get up.

"Excess," Stat said. "Some were greedy in life, while others were extravagant. The miserly and the wasteful are punished alike, for both show more concern for the earthly life than for the heavenly afterlife."

"How is this different from Hell?" Teddy asked. "People are punished for their sins in both places, so why is Purgatory any better?"

Stat let out a long sigh and explained, "These people are not being punished, not in the strict sense of the word. They are being purged of their sins. The souls in Hell have no hope for redemption, but these souls may rise to a higher level, and some may reach the lowest level of Heaven."

"What's the point of rising to a higher level, if it's just another place of punishment?"

"You weren't paying attention in church, were you? We are all guilty of all sins. If you had a thought in your head or a desire in your heart, you are as guilty as if you had acted on it."

Darkness was beginning to fall again, so Stat pulled out his blanket to cover them.

"We aren't going to be stuck here, are we?" Teddy asked.

"Not yet. You aren't dead."

Teddy shivered with apprehension, as did Candy, although neither of them could think of any excess they had committed. That fear seemed to come from their deep unconscious realization that they had another life in another time, in an extravagant mansion in Berkeley, California. Teddy began hearing the feminine voice inside his head, and she kept repeating, "It's all in your mind." He began to fall under the spell of Lorelei's voice and to hope that Candy was all in his mind, that he could spend eternity with his true soul mate. As dearly as his love for Candy had grown, he still felt that Lorelei was his proper soul mate, the one who could rescue him from the veil of illusion and lift him into the pure reality of Heaven.

#

Edna knew that her mother couldn't understand, but it still hurt to hear her husband criticized. Regardless of the chill that had enshrouded their relationship in recent years, she still loved him dearly, and perhaps more deeply than she had when the passion had still burned as a fire in her soul. She felt his pain, shared his suffering and even considered his antics at the amusement park original and creative, not at all harmful or embarrassing. Yes, it had been naughty of him to sneak into that room, but it was also quite a delicious break from the phony pomp and ceremony. Robert always had the ability to make her laugh, and that was more important than money, power or breeding. She prayed every night and every waking moment for her husband to wake up and come back to her.

She dreamed of strange places – pyramids in the desert, tropical forests, mountains inhabited by people who suffered the tortures of the dammed. She dreamed of climbing up a tree to build a nest for herself, finding her whole body covered with feathers, but that was okay because Robert was with her, and he also was covered with feathers.

The checks had started to come in for his music, his serious compositions, so their financial position wasn't quite as dire, but that income wasn't nearly as much as he had earned from the movies. She knew that she could no longer afford to keep the mansion. Reluctantly, she put it up for sale. Strolling through her beloved gardens, she said goodbye to every plant, one at a time, before leaving her home of ten years to move into a condominium apartment in town. She thought that she saw a raccoon lurking among the hydrangeas near the front porch.

Rob would like that, she knew. He had begged her to take an apartment instead of a huge, expensive house. She wouldn't miss the golden staircase or the marble pillars, but she would so miss the gardens that it broke her heart. She moved out in order to be away when the auction took place, and for that reason she was not there when the mansion was hit in a paramilitary-style raid, which left the doors knocked off of their hinges, the huge picture window smashed in, doors and cupboards rifled and all of the food from the refrigerator dumped out in a slimy mess on the kitchen floor.

The moving men had their van packed and ready to go, and a dealer had arrived to examine the remaining furniture, fine china and sterling to set prices for the auction. She hated to part with some of those things, but they simply would not fit into the small apartment in town. Besides, even with her lowered standard of living, she was going to need plenty of money to pay for her husband's rehabilitation. Even though the doctors had grown pessimistic, she refused to lose faith. He was going to wake up, and she was going to give him the care that he needed. Climbing into Angelica's little Toyota Camry, she rode to her new home with her daughter, thank God for her daughter, since she couldn't see to drive with all those tears stinging her eyes.

"It's okay, Mom, I'll teach you how to cook."

Edna let out a laugh, but she continued to weep.

"The apartment will be much easier to clean, and you'll have neighbors to keep you company."

"It's so hard to leave!"

"You're only leaving things, Mom. It's people that count."

"It isn't the big house, it's my gardens! Don't you know how often I worked in them myself, digging in the dirt with my own hands? I loved those gardens, so full of life and beauty."

"I'm so sorry. But you can visit the Arboretum, can't you?"

"It won't be the same. They won't be MY gardens."

Angelica gained a moment of insight. "You're really missing the vineyard, aren't you?"

"Yes!" Edna came to the realization in that moment, one that she had been denying for her entire adult life, that she wanted to go home. She wanted to be a child again. She wanted to start her life over and make better decisions, do things right this time. *Unfortunately*, she said to herself, *you can't go back.*

Only one part of the move had been easy, and that was telling Timothy that he had to go. The mansion was no longer his free crash pad, and she had no room for him at her apartment. She had no idea where the fat slob had gone, and she didn't care. The bum hadn't even once bothered to visit Robert in the hospital, or even to ask how he was doing.

#

Chapter Eleven

"Why are there only seven circles here?" Candy asked. "Hell had nine circles."

"Seven deadly sins," Stat explained.

"Oh."

"Then why nine circles in Hell?" Teddy asked.

"Have you ever heard," Stat patiently explained, "the expression that there's a special place in Hell?"

He offered no further explanation, and Candy and Teddy asked no further questions.

"I can take you up the next two levels, but I cannot lift you up to Paradise. That is beyond my power. Are you two ready to climb again?"

"I sure am," Teddy said. "I'm so hungry, I could eat a bug."

Candy giggled. "You did eat a bug, remember?"

"That wasn't me. I mean, I was not myself when I did that."

"Then who were you?"

Teddy stumbled around for an answer, but he couldn't find one.

"Stop it, you two," Stat commanded. It's time to proceed."

They followed him up to the sixth terrace, a lofty elevation near the clouds, with air so thin that they had to stop every few feet to sit down and suck in air. When they finally reached level ground, they saw a huge banquet table laid out before them, covered with all sorts of delicacies. They saw a dazzling array of roast pheasant, rack of lamb, oysters on ice, sliced quail eggs spread with caviar, fruits carved to look like floral arrangements, chocolate candies, caramel onions, cups of Darjeeling tea, pots of gourmet coffee, all with aromas that they could smell from six feet away, and every time they thought something was missing, it appeared on the banquet table. Ice cream, sherbet, stuffed potatoes, turkey with dressing, candied yams, all sorts of treats appeared as soon as they thought of them. The tantalizing aromas were too much for Teddy to bear. He began running toward the feast, while Candy called after him to stop.

"It's a trick!" she shouted. "Don't touch it!"

He ignored her, following the emptiness of his gut to the sumptuous meal in front of his eyes.

Suddenly, a big hand grabbed him by the shoulder and pulled him back. "Didn't you learn anything?" Stat asked, sounding exasperated. "This is exactly how you failed the test."

"But I'm so hungry," he complained.

"This food will not satisfy your hunger. It will only increase it. Leave it be."

Feeling miserable, Teddy fell in beside Candy to follow their guide through this level of Purgatory. Candy slid her arm inside his and gently nudged him. "Things are not as they appear," she whispered in his ear. Hearing those words, he thought again of Lorelei, and how he had married the wrong woman and lost all hope of ever being with his true soul mate. It was depressing to be so physically hungry for food and so emotionally hungry for love, at the same time.

As they walked around this circle, they saw thin wraiths milling around and moaning, speaking of their cravings for food and drink.

"Gluttons in life," Stat said, "they now must hunger for salvation."

"I still don't see how this is not punishment," Teddy complained. "These people are suffering, just as much as those in Hell."

"No, not nearly as much. Not for eternity, but only for a fixed time."

"It isn't fair. I mean, they're only human. We're all only human, with all the faults that go along with being human. Our species is subject to all the same needs as any other animal. We hunger, thirst and feel pain. We get tired, we want things, we lust after the opposite sex. It is natural for us to feel those things."

"Is it not also natural for the soul to refrain from acting on those feelings?" Stat stood still, and they almost walked right into his back. He seemed to be considering an idea that had just now occurred to him.

"Are we just going to stand around here?" Candy asked. "I'm cold and I'm hungry. And so is Teddy."

"You are not yet ready to pass through the curtain of fire." Stat disappeared in a cloud of smoke, and then the world around them began to dissolve as if it were merely a sand painting being washed away by ocean waves.

Candy screamed, and Teddy reached out to her, but his hand began dissolving into a multi-colored mass of pixels. He shouted her name, but he saw that she, too, was dispersing into millions of little colored dots. He screamed, even though he felt no pain. The last thing the two of them heard was each other's screams.

#

Mother Iris came into Father Diep's room in the basement of the sanctuary, where he was sitting on the edge of his bed and staring at the wall. The middle-aged woman carried herself with an air of authority befitting her high position in the Church. Taking the priest by the hand, she said, "Come with me. It is time for you to rest and recover from your labor."

The exhausted, disheveled priest followed her as a child follows his mother, relieved that his work was done but worried that he might not have accomplished his goal. She led him up the stairs into the Church proper, where she placed a white candle on the altar and handed him a match. As he lit the candle, Father Diep felt a great weight lifted from him.

"Did I succeed? Did he find his way?" he asked.

"Only the Lord knows, and now he is in the Lord's care. It is time for you to take care of yourself, and then you may resume your duties to the congregation." She put her arm on his shoulder and patted it. Her great old age showed in the purple veins that creased the wrinkled skin on her arm, and in the lines of her face, but her inner strength shone through her frail frame, making her appear youthful and ageless.

#

The alien implant, its batteries almost dead, found itself in a bin with the other toxic waste at the hospital. Exploring its surroundings, it found all sorts of edible tissues, plus several substances that glowed in the dark. After eating its fill, the implant began searching for a way out of the bin. The clasps on the outside kept the lid tightly seated on its plastic seals, but that was no problem. It simply chewed through the seals with the sharp beak in the center of its bottom orifice and reached out its tentacles through the space that it had opened up to unfasten the latches. From the outside a raccoon helped, working the clasp with its thumbless black hands. Unfortunately, it waddled away without lifting the lid, which was still too heavy for the slug to push up from the inside.

This process took several days, as the implant had to figure out what was keeping it inside this hermetically sealed container before it could implement the solution. Once out in the hallway, it tried to signal the alien ship for new instructions, but the flying saucer had traveled beyond the solar system by now and the implant's batteries were too weak to broadcast a signal strong enough to reach them. Left on its own, it began roaming the hallways, always avoiding the strange bipedal creatures that rushed aimlessly to and fro, threatening to squash it with their clumsy feet. They didn't seem to take any notice of the implant as it explored the hospital in search of water. Slugs must have water, or they dry up and die. It took to slithering across the ceiling, which was the one place where it was safe from stomping feet and crashing carts. When it came to operating in this strange world, the implant was as blind as an owl in daylight.

It felt the need to bond with another bipedal creature, as it had been bonded when the alien slugs created it. As a symbiote, it would become the Conduit, not merely a mass of gut sliding along painted surfaces, but a channel for the processing of information. The implant had so many ideas running through its brain, thoughts of sin and punishment, heroic deeds and love affairs, that it desperately needed the means to express those symbols in stories and give birth to their manifestation as real objects in the physical world. The reification of its ideas, the hypostasis of information, seemed the highest ambition to which any creature might aspire. After taking a long drink in a white porcelain bowl, it began to examine the various bipedal creatures who lay in beds and therefore might be easy targets for bonding. It had no way of knowing that it had wandered into the mental ward.

#

Robert Wells awoke from his dreams of another life with a dull ache inside his head, itching where his hair had started to grow back around the site of the surgery and little memory of who he had been before the mugging. Strangers in white uniforms walked him to the toilet, cleaned him, groomed him and dressed him. Nearly everything was done for him because he could not remember how to do anything. They lifted spoons of food to his mouth and wiped his chin with paper napkins. For an hour every day, they made him try to walk. Even with the four-legged walker to help him, he had trouble moving his feet without falling down. He began to experience his body as a wonderful animal that carried him through this life, bearing his burdens, pains and sorrows. This animal was separate from himself but bonded to him as a partner and an equal.

One day two women arrived. They seemed familiar to him, but he wasn't sure who they were. When they asked him did he want to go home, he repeated the word, "Home." He wasn't sure what it meant, but it had a pleasant sound to it and he liked the way his mouth made a round shape when he said it, so he kept on repeating that one word, "Home." Soon he found himself rolled out in a wheelchair to a waiting taxi cab. Two of the white-uniformed people who had been caring for him lifted him up and slid him into the back seat. The familiar women got in on either side of him, and soon the cab was rolling down the streets of a city. The women talked the whole way, perhaps to each other or perhaps to him, but he couldn't understand most of what they said, so he remained silent. A smile creased his lips when he stared at the younger woman. She reminded him of someone he had once loved more dearly than life itself. He couldn't remember her name, but for now it was enough that he could look at her and adore her. The older woman began to look more familiar, too, and he felt certain that he had some kind of relationship with her, but it felt painful. So he turned away and gazed at the younger woman, the one who made him feel warm and squishy inside.

When the younger woman and the cab driver walked him through the front door of a ground-floor apartment and sat him down on the sofa, he knew that he never had been in this place before, even though he remembered the sofa from his dim and murky past. It was terribly confusing, but he lacked the means to do anything about it. In fact, his language skills weren't even good enough to ask the others about it. He would have to wait until things became more clear in his mind. His legs still felt rubbery, and he had walked like a drunk. Yes, he remembered what drunk meant. There was no way that he could walk on his own, without others helping. He would have to sit here and wait for others to move him.

For now, he felt comfortable enough on the soft cushions, so he relaxed and examined his surroundings. To the left of the sofa, he saw a heavily curtained window, and in front of the window stood a heavy brown chair that looked uncomfortable. He thought that he could make out the shadow of a raccoon behind the curtains. To the right and behind him, he saw an open doorway leading into a hall. He assumed that the bedrooms and bathroom would be found in that direction. Farther to his right, he saw a small open area with a tiny dining table. The top of the table was cheap yellow Formica, and four equally cheap green plastic chairs stood around the table. This little dining area led into the kitchen, a cramped rectangle that was dominated by a white refrigerator and a brown stove. He didn't like the fact that the colors didn't match. In fact, they weren't even coordinated. The younger woman was standing by the stove, stirring a pot of soup. He hoped that it was tomato bisque and that she would bring him a grilled cheese sandwich with a mug of that soup.

In front of him, against the opposite wall, stood a huge flat-screen television set, flanked on either side by bookcases. The television screen was blank, since the set had not been turned on, but he stared at it in anticipation of something that he could not define. Robert felt that he was waiting for something, for some kind of instructions. Someone would send him a signal that would disinhibit his mind. The screen across the room would burst into life, beaming a message directly to him, and then the gray clouds would disappear from his thinking, the dullness give way to brightness and his mind become free to think and speak and act.

The older woman was holding a little electronic gadget up to her ear and talking to it, as if she were holding a conversation with another person. After a few pleasantries, she shrieked.

"No!" Edna cried out. "Are there any suspects? Did they wreck everything? I really *need* the money from the auction."

"It's mostly the house that was damaged," Harold Silver told her. The head of the auction house, who had found the mess and reported it to the police, carried out the difficult task of informing the owner of the mansion. He was used to this sort of thing, vandals and burglars targeting empty houses, but of course Edna Wells was not used to such things. "The doors and the picture window will need to be repaired, and the kitchen needs to be cleaned up," he said. "But nothing seems to be missing. It must have been some teenagers blowing off steam. Professional burglars would have taken the paintings and the silver."

"I'll be glad when the house is sold," Edna told him. "Then I won't have to worry about such things."

"What I don't understand," Harold told her, "is why your security system didn't alert the police. It seems to be working properly now, but it failed to detect the break-in."

"I'll call the alarm company right away," she said, "and let them know that their system malfunctioned. And then I'll call my insurance company."

The strangest thing about the burglary at the mansion was the presence of a white powder all over the carpets in the upstairs bedrooms. The second strangest thing was the food dumped out of the refrigerator. What could they have been looking for? Kids just going wild made more sense than any other explanation. Still, it was weird. And they apparently used some kind of explosives on the unlocked storage cabinet where Robert Wells used to keep his books and papers. Edna had already packed up all of them, including his original compositions, and stashed them in the bedroom closet at her apartment.

At that moment, her husband spoke his first complete sentence since the surgery. "There was a Conduit," he said.

Edna hurriedly got off the telephone, hanging up on Harold Silver while he was still saying goodbye, and sat down beside her husband on the sofa. "Yes, Dear? You were saying?" She took his hand in hers.

Hardly seeming to notice her, he said, "I've lost the Conduit." Staring at the opposite wall, he tried to form a mental picture of the Conduit. He could see nothing, but he could feel an emptiness in the back of his head. Yes, that was it. They had removed the Conduit in the white room. The blank white wall opposite him began to shimmer like a curtain of water. He blinked his eyes several times, but his vision did not clear up. He felt a terrible emptiness, the loneliness of a twin who has lost his twin, lost half of his own soul. In fact, he concluded that he must have sold his soul to the Devil, and that the Devil had come to collect.

"Talk to me," Edna urged.

Robert spoke, but not to her. "The veil is being lifted," he said. "Sophia is returning."

"Who is Sophia?" Edna asked. "I don't think I know her.

Still ignoring her, Robert stared at the television across the room and continued talking to some person or presence who remained totally invisible to his wife. "We must correct the errors which have injured her and clouded our vision."

Their medical insurance provided a home health care nurse who came in every day to spend four hours teaching Robert Wells to walk, talk, feed himself and go to the bathroom. Without that small blessing, Edna might have gone insane. When her daughter went back to school, it was just the two of them. She hadn't planned on having a two-year-old for a husband, and that was just about what she had. It was bad enough that she had to take a job as a secretary at the newspaper office, without having to raise a six-foot, 200-pound child at the same time. Knowing that her husband would try to put the make on any woman, even his nurse, she specified that the nurse must be at least middle aged and happily married. The agency didn't even blink at this demand, since most wives had the same list of requirements.

After the nurse had gone for the day, Robert spent most of his time sitting on the sofa and staring at the television set, never bothering to pick up the remote control and change the channel, even though Edna set the device in his lap. He didn't even turn the set on, but instead sat there staring at it until someone else turned it on for him. He didn't talk much, and when he did speak, he seemed to be having a conversation with a philosopher or theologian whom nobody else could see.

#

In a condominium apartment just a few miles away, a lovely woman packed her things into cardboard boxes and stashed them in the trunk and the back seat of her car. All that she knew of her former keeper was what she had heard on the evening news, and that wasn't much. He had been mugged, hospitalized, seemingly recovered, and seemingly forgotten all about her. The one fact with which she must deal was that his monthly checks no longer arrived, so she could no longer remain in his little love nest. Breathing in the crisp morning air as she packed up her Dodge Intrepid for the trip home to her mother's house, she felt a strange sense of freedom, as if chains had been removed from her limbs. For the first time in years, she was free to make her own decisions, although she no longer had the financial means to do some of the things to which she had become accustomed. No more eating out at fancy restaurants, no more shopping binges for designer clothing and jewelry, but also no more slavery, no more being at the beck and call of a lonely, lovesick puppy of a man.

#

Messenger Josiah frowned, showing his displeasure. "We must find it," he said.

"We will find it, Sir," Lieutenant Azazel assured him.

"These things are dangerous, and they must not be allowed to live."

"Yes, Sir."

"It must be found, and it must be killed." The Messenger pounded his fist on the desk for emphasis. "This could destroy the very fabric of civilization."

The two men sat in a secret office in a nondescript building somewhere in Colorado, Messenger Josiah in the large red chair behind the desk and Lieutenant Azazel in the small gray chair facing the desk. The men wore no uniforms, so insignia of rank. To the outside world, they were computer programmers working for an Internet company. Within their own circles, they were troubleshooters ensuring that the wheels of society rolled smoothly.

"We all know that, Sir. We've been briefed."

They all knew that the flying saucer which had landed near the film production studio was not an advertising balloon. In fact, they had concocted that cover story, themselves. They had hoped to capture and sterilize the crew of that craft, but before they had their equipment in place, it had escaped and gone back to whatever solar system it had come from. They knew for a fact, however, that it had left behind a most interesting and potentially dangerous device. The Agency had already wasted enormous resources searching for the alien craft, and after it had flown away, sending out a clean-up team in hazardous materials suits that resembled outrageous beekeepers' outfits, taking samples of the soil and vegetation in and around the hole that the flying saucer had left behind and then cleaning up the site to remove all trace of the alien presence. At least their search of the amusement park had cost them little more than the price of admission. The men had found it easy to blend in with the other tourists and take readings with their detectors.

"Do you really know? Do you really understand? The whole system upon which the world depends could fall apart if this thing got into the wrong hands. The information that it imparts to the uninitiated, the power that it would give them, is more dangerous than a thermonuclear bomb. This is not merely a Communist plot. It is as much anti-Communist as it is anti-American. This thing will destroy the whole fabric of society, if we don't manage to stop it right here, right now!"

"It definitely was not in the mansion, Messenger," Lieutenant Azazel said. "So now the hospital is being searched. Discretely, of course."

"And the apartment? There's always the possibility that he still has it with him."

"That's next on our list."

The Messenger waved his hand, and they left the room. He studied the latest report from the outside detective agency that he had hired to follow Robert Wells. Following him was a metaphoric term for sitting outside his apartment in case he went out, which he never did. He already had everything on the subject that could be retrieved from the computer database. It seemed highly unlikely that a third-rate musician would engage in subversive activities, and yet Wells most definitely had the device in his possession at some point in time, and that device was the most subversive mechanism in the universe.

#

Kelvin Jaggle stood on the street corner holding a white poster-board sign on which he had written with chisel-tipped permanent red marker, "DISCLOSURE IS IMMINENT, HYPOSTASIS IN THE TRUE MIND". That summation of the hypothesis would be easily recognized by those who possessed gnosis, and it ought to spark the beginnings of knowledge in those who lacked it.

He recited his thesis for hours, often repeating himself, seemingly unaware when passersby stopped to listen and when they walked away, shaking their heads in amusement or disapproval. Most of the passersby paid little attention to the tall, thin man with ragged yellow hair and dark, piercing eyes. He continued trying to reach them, the sleepers who walked through life in a somnambulant state, unaware that they were prisoners in a slave labor camp. The message was everything, and he knew for a certainty that the right people would hear his message and gain the knowledge that would set them free from this illusory world. They would begin to see through the prison of stone blocks and iron bars, into the true reality that lay beyond illusion. He had learned this in the hospital, when the Other melded its mind with his, but he had been cagey enough to keep the secret hidden from the controllers with their clipboards and pills and group therapy sessions. Those minions of the Demiurge had been fooled into releasing him, believing that he had finally been made to conform to the shared reality of their system. They had no idea that he could see through the veil of their koinos kosmos into the true reality.

The two organisms, now symbiotically fused into one, became a new species: *Homo conduitus sapiens*. The implant had helped him to pass their draconian tests. When they showed him cartoons on plastic cards, it helped him to make up a story about parents who loved their children and taught them a lesson. When he took the multiple choice test, it advised him not to admit that he could see and hear things that others did not. When they confronted him with the dreaded proverbs, it helped him to interpret them in the accepted ways, as wise metaphors and not simply nuggets of concrete fact. In spite of that, he still could not make any sense out of "a new broom sweeps clean". It seemed to him that an old broom would do just as well. And the rolling stone, well, he thought that moss was bad, so he found it incomprehensible when the implant told him to say that you need to stay still in order to get good things like friendship. But he dutifully mouthed the words that the implant fed him, in order to convince the doctors to release him.

Now that he had his freedom, he was eager to resume his missionary work. His old message had been only a part of the new Truth that the Conduit was about to expose. The world had to know about the Messengers and the Demiurge and the Prison of Illusion which they had imposed upon the children of God. He produced a brochure on the computer at the public library, and he had printed out three dozen copies before they made him stop, pointing out that ink and paper cost money. He offered them a dollar that he had in his pocket, rendering unto Caesar, but apparently they didn't want him using their ink and paper, even if he paid for them. They simply wouldn't allow him to print any more copies. In fact, they asked him to leave and not to come back until he had bathed and put on clean clothes. So he stood on the street corner and recited the contents of his brochure, as well as any other thoughts that came into his mind. The brochures, all but one that he kept for himself, he placed on the windshields of parked cars at the local Q-Mart.

At first he wondered why other people couldn't see the stone blocks and iron bars of their prison. They lived in ignorance, falsely believing themselves free, when in fact they were enslaved. But then the Conduit showed him the black veils that covered their faces, the finest spider webs of black lace obscuring their vision, blinding them to the truth. They couldn't understand their situation any more than an owl could see in daylight. In fact, they were walking in their sleep, only partially conscious. The seed of gnosis lay dormant in their minds.

"Sleepers, awake!" he shouted. Then in a quiet voice, he spoke the truth. "The Empire never ended. It simply took on another form, a different outward appearance. God is in the trash cans, salvation in the gutters. Open your eyes and see the world as it truly is, not as it appears to be. The living die, and the dead live. There's a bad moon rising on December 21, 2012. What was will be, and what is will not be.

We live in an ersatz reality, the construct of the system which imprisons us and controls our minds. All of the objects in our world are faulty replications of the true forms in the hyperreality. Rome gave the masses bread and circuses. Today the Empire gives us food stamps and television."

After pausing to sip his McDonald's coffee, he shouted to a well-dressed woman who was trying to ignore him, "Have you ever been to Disneyland?"

Reflexively, and to her regret, the woman turned her head and looked at him.

"That's right, Madame, I said Disneyland. Now, there's the ultimate faux reality. Amusement park rides, attractions and fireworks. Junk food served on plastic plates with plastic forks, paper napkins and plastic cups. And yet, behind that façade is the reality: Disneyland really is a park, Lady."

The woman had scurried away from this unwanted attention, but Jaggle continued his harangue as if she were still there, listening attentively.

"Behind all that fluff, Disneyland is filled with plants and trees, squirrels and birds and other animals. It is a nature preserve, underneath the plastic coating. Yet the people who go there never see it. All that meets their eyes is the glitz of the manufactured world."

Spotting a police car prowling its way toward him through the rush-hour traffic on Shattuck Avenue, Jaggle turned his sign around and tucked it under his arm. He knew better than to try talking sense to the servants of the Demiurge. They would lock him up again, and he would have to fool the doctors into letting him out again. He had no time for such nonsense, as the time was growing short. He found it easy enough to blend in with the other pedestrians and slip into the darkness of a movie theatre. He couldn't believe the price of the ticket, ten dollars! At that price, they'd better let him spend the night there, since he didn't have enough money left for a cheap motel room. His next disability check wasn't due for three more days, and it never was enough to get him through the month, no matter how frugally he lived.

He wasn't much into movies, but he thought that they provided a meaningful metaphor for the world. A mere trick of the light led people to believe that they were seeing real people, places, things and events, rather than the shadows and reflections that struck the screen from an unseen projector kept always behind the audience.

After the usual commercial ads and previews, the movie finally began. The opening credits rolled over the scene of a man jogging on a dirt path around a small lake in a city park. A few feet away, a large German shepherd ran between the trees, pacing the jogger and perhaps hunting him down. The title of the movie came up in blood-red letters dripping down the screen: *Bad Moon Rising*. An adolescent girl looked into the bathroom mirror and screamed. Instead of her own lovely face, the mirror showed a wolf snarling, its white fangs gleaming, saliva dripping from its jaws. He made a mental note that mirrors could show a person's true soul, that which lay behind the mask.

The movie turned out to be a cheap teen slasher flick, filled with gore, but somehow the music resonated with something inside his head. Kelvin Jaggle, bored by the predicable plot, dozed off and entered into dreams of incantations, potions and contracts signed in blood. When he awoke, the closing credits were rolling over the scene of a wolf pack running through a wooded area. Apparently that was a happy ending, since the music was rising in a major key; it sounded happy, anyway.

The implant enjoyed this new host, in no small part due to the fact that it had managed to seat itself in the higher centers of the brain, instead of the autonomic nerve center and the locus of instincts and reflexes. This new situation allowed it access to, and communication with, the reasoning part of the brain of its new host. Having no way to reestablish the connection with the amusement park's computer without the help of the alien slugs, it persuaded the host to find a computer that it could access. This led to many hours in the public library, pouring through the databases of Lexus Nexus and a variety of abstracts from scientific journals. The new host kept reading books and articles about UFOs and alien encounters, something which the implant found tedious and boring. The bipedal creatures inhabiting this planet seemed to have a vast mythology about space aliens, most of which was pure fantasy.

Now it sought to find this host a bath and clean clothes, so the librarians would let them back in. The implant needed more information to quench its insatiable thirst for knowledge. Without guidance from the alien slugs, it followed its internal program, which called for information processing.

#

Searching the hospital had been relatively easy, although fruitless, for the minions. The staff paid little attention to people in white uniform coats or green scrubs, and even security didn't bother to look closely at the ID badges pinned to their shirt pockets. The various detection devices failed to turn up anything more interesting than pellets of radioactive substances used in cancer treatment. The alien device simply was not in the hospital. This meant that they must search the apartment, and that would be a little more complicated. The Messengers preferred to conduct their searches while nobody was at home, but the invalid never left the apartment. Surveillance tapes showed him sitting on the sofa all day, staring at the television set. It didn't seem to matter whether the set was on or off; he still sat there staring at it until somebody walked him into the bedroom and tucked him in. They would have to invent some reason to get him out of the house. A follow-up visit to the hospital seemed like the safest bet, so they contacted a doctor on the staff who had been known to cooperate with them in the past. This time they took pains to leave everything as they had found it, to leave behind no clue that they ever had been there. The raid on the mansion had been sloppy, but they deemed it acceptable because that residence was unoccupied at the time. The apartment, on the other hand, must be thoroughly cleaned and sanitized before they left.

Despite all their careful planning and a thorough search, they failed to turn up the alien device. Then some genius suggested that the tumor which had been removed from Robert Wells WAS the device. Since hospitals kept detailed records, it should be easy to find out what they had done with it.

#

Robert Wells sat on the edge of the examination table, dressed in a green cloth robe that hung open at the back, while a white-coated intern tested his reflexes and looked at his eyes, ears and throat. Wells had regained most of his language skills, but he felt totally unmotivated when it came to communicating with the medical staff. He felt that it was enough for him to follow their instructions, without trying to engage them in conversation. They could tell him nothing about the Conduit, anyway; such knowledge lay outside their field. While they poked and prodded and took notes, he was busy mentally composing an opera, something like Mozart's *The Magic Flute*, but instead of revealing the secrets of the Masonic order, he planned to set the secrets of the universe to music. His hero would be trapped behind the iron bars of a prison, seeking to escape in order to bring the true gnosis to his friends.

The story was just beginning to take shape in his mind, and he felt that he would need a professional librettist. After all, his education was in music, not literature. Despite his doubts about his ability to write a story, he did feel that he had enough ideas to write down notes and an outline as soon as he could get his hands on a pen and a pad of paper. The secret knowledge would unfold gradually, beginning with the mustard seed of truth. We see only dim reflections of the real world. The universe is a darkened room filled with funhouse mirrors. We walk through life as through a maze, confronted occasionally with distorted reflections of ourselves which we take for strangers. Whatever we do to them, we do to ourselves. Wachet auf! Wake up! We are all asleep and suffering from the shared nightmare of an artificial world created by the Demiurge to keep us imprisoned. We are all enslaved to the false god of this world.

The phrase "cryptica scriptura" kept running through his mind, but he couldn't quite grasp what it was supposed to mean. He never had been particularly religious, although he had attended church once or twice a year. Divorced from the implant, he was forced to depend upon his own feeble intellectual faculties to sort through the jumble of images that haunted his reverie and find the thread of meaning within the chaos.

He felt relief when the home health nurse and his wife Edna finally led him into the apartment and sat him down on the sofa. The television screen sparked into life and showed him the evening news, a jumble of death, war and other tragedies, plus the failing world economy. The newscasters terrified him, and he sat stone still, frozen with fear. The handsome man and the pretty woman in their business suits looked human enough, but they couldn't hide their lizard eyes and their darting tongues as they read the news off of the teleprompter. He often caught glimpses of the reality behind the appearance, such as these obvious reptilian aliens masquerading as human. He had seen the same lizard eyes on the face of the doctor at the hospital, and that also frightened him.

Rob was able to take care of himself well enough to stay home alone while Edna went to work, and so he was alone the next day when something remarkable happened. He was sitting on the sofa as usual, watching the television set and writing notes of whatever thoughts crossed his mind, when he distinctly heard the voices of the newscasters telling him to kill himself.

"You're no good," the woman said.

"You're a waste of space," the man chimed in.

"You should eliminate yourself. The world will be a better place without you." The woman's reptilian eyes squinted, as if to see Rob more clearly through the glass of the television screen.

For the first time, he realized that he could control the television and felt motivated to do so. Picking up the remote that lay on the cushion beside him, he changed the channel. Another news broadcast appeared on the screen, and another pair of beautiful news readers started chanting at him, "You should die, you should kill yourself."

He turned the set off, and the picture disappeared, but he could still hear them chanting at him. He got up and walked to the bathroom, where he splashed cold water on his face until he thought that his mind had cleared. He felt that he was obviously suffering from some kind of hallucination, no doubt an after-effect of the trauma of being mugged and then going through brain surgery. He could still hear the voices, although they had grown fainter, so he went into the bedroom and shut the door. This seemed as good a time as any to take a nap. As he crawled under the covers, he began to hear a faint buzzing sound that seemed to be coming from inside his ears. He laid his head on the pillow and closed his eyes. The buzzing sound gradually grew louder, until he thought that he couldn't stand it any more. He decided to get up and make himself a cup of coffee, but his limbs refused to obey him. He lay flat on his back, helpless, unable to move, unable even to shout for help. Then he realized that nobody was at home to help him, anyway.

#

Chapter Twelve

Timothy sat in the outer office of Messenger Josiah, pleading with the secretary to let him into the inner office. He had dressed in his best silk suit, and he even wore a color-coordinated green-and-blue diagonally striped tie to set off the teal jacket. He felt extremely uncomfortable with his neck corseted in the knotted tie and his belly confined in a vest that had gradually, over the years become too tight. "But I've earned an audience," he pleaded. "Look, it's all here in his chart. All of the stars and planets are showing that – well, that's something only for the ears of the Messenger." He shoved the sheaf of papers back into the 8 by 10 manila envelope and sealed it, peeling off the strip of paper and discarding it on the carpeted floor besides his chair. He saw no sense in being courteous to the ill-mannered secretary, so he didn't bother to pick up his trash.

The secretary, a shallow-chested man with a greasy complexion, raised a skeptical eyebrow. "The Messenger is much too busy to see anyone today. If you will leave the papers with me –"

"Never!" Timothy cut him off. "Would I leave a gourmet dinner in the care of a dog?" Most of his metaphors had to do with food, the most important thing in his life, as attested to by his round belly.

"I assure you, Sir," the secretary intoned with an air of disdain, "that I never presume to read any of the Messenger's private correspondence. Now, will you leave the papers on my desk, or will you take them with you?" The secretary pressed a button on the underside of his desk, and two big men in black suits entered the room. "This gentleman was just leaving," he told them.

"All right!" Timothy stood up and slammed the 8 by 10 manila envelope down on the desk. "But these charts are for the eyes of the Messenger only! If you break the seal, he will know it."

The two big men took their positions on either side of him and walked with him through the lobby, through the glass doors leading outside the building and across the parking lot, all the way to his car, a beat-up old Subaru Justy with a stick shift and a three-cylinder, two-stroke engine.

"Would you like a ride?" he asked sarcastically. "I could take you downtown to buy some decent clothes."

The men stood silent, glaring at him but refusing to respond to his taunt. Timothy backed the car up and rolled down his window. "Have a nice day!" he shouted, then started forward so abruptly that the tires squealed. He wondered what was so special about this Messenger, that he never deigned to meet face-to-face with the people who worked for him.

He had worked for years on his brother-in-law's star charts, plotting each significant moment in his life, refining the calculations after he pinned down the exact time and place of Robert Wells' birth. He lined up the past alignments with the significant events, constantly referring to the latest astronomical observations of planets, stars, asteroids and comets, developing the most detailed and complete chart humanly possible. Then he accomplished the most difficult task of plotting future significant events in Robert Wells' life. The Messenger had requested it, and Timothy had delivered it, and still he was not allowed to meet his master.

A week later, a check arrived in the mail. Alliance Software paid him a measly ten thousand dollars for the work of five years. Five years since his ex-wife had begged Robert with her dying breath to take care of Timothy, the helpless victim of a lack of education, coupled with a lack of motivation. Timothy, the helpless victim of circumstances whom Edna his double-crossing sister had thrown out on the street as soon as she had the opportunity to do so, in the absence of her convalescent husband.

#

Robert Wells lay helpless, flat on his back in bed, unable to move or speak, while some unseen entity projected a motion picture onto the bedroom ceiling. He saw himself as a young boy, as a teenager, as a young adult. *This must be the life review*, he thought, *that you have to watch before you die. I must be dying.* The thought of his own death did not frighten him; in fact, he thought that it would be a relief, after being forced to watch all of his past sins.

The film showed them all, from the time that he shoplifted a candy bar from Bixby's corner market, to the time he cheated on his wife – all the times, that is, that he cheated on his wife. Those glimpses went by far too quickly, perhaps because he was enjoying them too much, in spite of the guilt. The final sin, before the life review ended, was his constant longing for Lorelei, a woman who looked all too familiar. Rob came to the conclusion that he deserved to die, since Lorelei looked so much like Angelica that he must have been lusting after his own daughter. Ignorantly or not, like Oedipus he had committed incest, and he must pay the price for it.

He would have slashed his wrists right then and there, if he had been able to move. Fortunately, his absolution was close at hand. He could hear Edna's key in the lock, the doorknob turning and the front door creaking open – somebody should oil the hinges, he thought, as if a squeaky door were the most important thing in the world.

Edna called out his name, and suddenly he was able to move again. He got up to see what she wanted.

"This is my friend Sophia, from work," Edna said.

"Edna has told me so much about you," Sophia said.

Rob stuttered, "I – I'm v- very gl- glad to m-meet you," he said. This new woman, Sophia, did not merely resemble Lorelei; she was an exact duplicate, like a clone or a Xerox copy. And when she spoke, that confirmed it; Sophia was Lorelei, and so he had not been lusting after his own daughter, after all. She was simply someone who resembled Angelica.

"Sophia is a reporter, and she's doing an article on people who've had brain surgery," Edna told him. "Would it be okay if she interviewed you? She won't use your real name, so it'll be anonymous."

"Unless," Sophia said, "you want me to use your real name. For publicity, I mean, to promote your music."

Rob felt so relieved that he had to sit down, but not on the sofa where he would be staring at the evil television set. "Let's have some coffee," he said, going to the dining table and plopping down on one of the green plastic chairs.

Sophia at down opposite him and set down her clipboard on the table, while Edna started up the coffee maker. "Now," she said, "let's start with before the surgery. Were you feeling anxious about it?"

"Yes, of course."

"And did the doctors or the nursing staff help in any way to soothe your misgivings or allay your fears?"

The interview went on for over an hour, and Rob thought the questions both infantile and boring, but he felt such relief at the epiphany he had just experienced, that he had been longing for a woman he never met before, that he didn't mind answering them. Besides, he enjoyed looking at this dark-haired beauty, listening to her melodic voice and realizing, finally, that he really did not want her in a romantic sense. In fact, the more he talked to her, the more he realized how badly he had needed to talk about the surgery and its aftereffects. It never occurred to him to talk to his wife about it, and Edna never asked him. She seemed to think that life should go on as before, or as nearly like before as possible, given their severely reduced financial circumstances.

When Sophia asked him about the surgery, he winced.

"That's kind of painful," Edna said, warming up their coffee with fresh, hot liquid from the glass carafe.

"It's okay if you don't want to answer," Sophia told him, with a sympathetic expression on her face.

"Well, really," he said, "all that I remember is waking up in the hospital bed with a dull ache in the back of my skull."

"What was it like when you came home?"

"it was strange to me, except for the furniture. You see, we didn't live here before. This dining set, for example, used to be our patio furniture. And the sofa was in one of the guest rooms."

"I see. So in a sense, you didn't really come home."

"In a sense, but actually, this apartment seems more like home than a big house ever could." He gazed into her eyes, and he foresaw that they would have a love affair, a steamy, passionate relationship. He imagined her with her blouse unbuttoned, the round tops of her breasts peeking out from under a pink satin bra.

Sophia frowned and shot him an icy glance, as if she had read his thoughts and disapproved. He felt sharp pangs in his belly, pangs of guilt, as if he had already cheated on his wife.

"Your wife has born a great deal of stress herself," Sophia said.

Edna nodded in agreement.

Sophia continued, "It isn't easy to see a loved one suffer, and it's also very difficult to care for an invalid in your home. And, of course, Edna never had to work before."

#

Later that evening, while Edna heated a TV dinner in the microwave – the closest thing to cooking that she could manage – Rob said, "I don't think you should work."

Edna stared at him for a moment and then said, "Who is going to pay our bills?"

"I don't know, but it just doesn't seem right for you to be gone all day. I mean, it must be hard for you, having to take care of everything."

"Yes, it is hard. But somebody has to do it."

The microwave beeped to a stop, and Edna opened the door to peel back the plastic film and stir the mashed potatoes before nuking the meal for another five minutes.

"I used to do that. Why can't I be the one who goes to work?"

"Because, for one thing, you've lost your driver's license and we can't afford to pay someone else to drive you around. And for another, you've turned down every job that comes your way."

"Those movies are garbage."

Edna sat down opposite her husband and stared directly into his eyes. "That didn't used to matter," she told him.

"Well, now it does. Can't we get by on my serious music?"

"Not if you want to pay the rent, keep the lights on and eat."

"Oh. Well, maybe I can go on a speaking tour, if I can figure out what to say. You did tell me that the colleges and universities want me to lecture to their music students."

Taking his hand in hers, she said, "We could try that. But you'll need to make a lot of speeches, if you want to pay the bills. They hardly offer enough money to make it worth the plane fare."

Rob spent the rest of the evening trying to compose a speech about the art and craft of music. It wasn't so much that he felt embarrassed about his wife supporting him, as that he worried that she might meet some other man and have a fling, a love affair. After all, that was what he had done, when he was the one who went to work and was out of the house all day.

#

Kelvin Jaggle exited the homeless shelter, where he had sought a hot meal and a warm bed on a cold night, dressed in a clean suit of clothes that were not too badly worn, his hair and beard neatly trimmed and combed, feeling almost naked after having scrubbed off several layers of dirt and dead skin in the shower. He liked the feel of the tan brushed cotton slacks, the clean shirt and quilted nylon jacket. The new socks and shoes put a spring into his step, giving him the energy to walk farther and with less foot pain than before, when he had marched around sockless in tattered leather loafers.

The shelter refused to keep him as a resident, beyond that one night when the cold temperature made it necessary to provide him with a cot and a blanket, since he was neither an alcoholic nor a drug addict. But the charitable people there had done what they could for him, even giving him twenty dollars before sending him on his way. He would need that money to buy new poster board and felt-tipped markers. His cardboard sign had crumpled into a soggy mess during yesterday's rain storm. As he walked down the streets of Skid Row, he picked up the occasional piece of trash lying on the sidewalk or in the gutter and stuffed it in to the backpack that they had given him. The Voice had told him that he would find

Darkening 225

messages in the trash, so he collected each piece, saving them all to study them later, once he found a safe place to sit down.

Now that he had bathed and put on clean clothes, he could return to the library. The problem was, he no longer knew how to find it. He had walked down so many streets, stood on so many corners holding up his sign and reciting his thesis, that he no longer knew where he was.

Worse, the Other had left him. It must have happened during the night, when he was asleep, since he hadn't noticed it leaving. But he no longer heard the guiding Voice, and that was why he kept on picking up the pieces of trash that caught his eye, hoping and yearning for guidance. He would have asked for directions to the library, but the obvious tweakers who inhabited this part of town gave him the shivers. He thought that he might have better luck with the hookers on the corner, but they demanded that he pay them for the information. So he kept on walking, and he kept on picking up trash and stuffing it into his backpack. He was anxious to get out of this area with its filthy sidewalks, wads of chewing gum and other, more disgusting substances, stuck to the concrete.

When he bent down to pick up a Doxima Chips wrapper, a shoe suddenly came down on top of it, preventing him from picking it up. Rising slowly, he discovered that the shoe belonged to a foot, and that the foot belonged to a big man in a black suit.

"We've been looking for you," the man said.

Jaggle couldn't resist the opening for a smart retort, so he said, "Yeah, you and who else?"

A black limousine with tinted windows pulled up alongside the curb, and the driver, also a big man in a black suit, got out and opened the back door on the passenger side. Without another word, the two men hustled Jaggle into the back seat and drove away with him.

#

The False Messengers found the process of screening potential carriers tedious and time-consuming. This irritated them no end, as they knew that they were already following a cold trail. Since they hadn't detected the device in the hospital, it had to have been carried out by one of the patients who had been released within a week after Robert Wells' surgery. Most had been easy to track down and check out, since they had fixed places of residence and many had returned for follow-up visits to their doctors. There was only this one man left, a derelict without a home, who failed to return to the hospital, and with good reason. He was a mental patient. The poor deluded soul actually believed himself free, just because he had left one ordered section of the system for another. Of course he didn't want to go back to the hospital, where he could clearly see the cage in which he was kept. Like a prisoner let out on parole, he had put as much distance as possible between himself and the place of his confinement. Tracking him down had been difficult, but not impossible. Interrogating Kelvin Jaggle turned out to be even more difficult. They had emptied out his backpack, finding nothing but trash, so they tossed it into the dumpster. Since the device was not in his possession, he must tell them where he had stashed it.

"Where is it?" the white-coated interrogator asked.

"Where is what?"

"The device. Where did you put it?"

"Everything I own is in the backpack, man. If you want something, go ahead and keep it. Just let me go."

"We want the device. You left it somewhere. Where did you leave it?"

Jaggle continued protesting his ignorance, even under drugs and hypnosis. They did learn where he had been since his release from the mental ward, and that was just about every street in the city of Berkeley. No matter what they tried, they failed to extract from him any knowledge of the device. He just kept babbling about the Other and how it had abandoned him in the homeless shelter. They continued relentlessly torturing him with cold showers and grating noises, but the man was obviously insane and incapable of understanding what they wanted. Eventually, they dumped the derelict out on the street near the hospital and sent out a crew to search the homeless shelter.

#

Chapter Thirteen

Robert Wells sat on the sofa taking notes, once again watching the television, this time looking not for messages from the Divine, but for signs of the evil forces that ruled this world. He saw a raccoon walk across the screen, then a woman's face appeared and began thinking to him. Her lips did not move, but he could hear her voice inside his head.

The experience of the previous day had hit him like a bolt of lightning, the brightest light he had ever seen entering his skull through the Third Eye, filling his pineal gland with the pure light of gnosis. For some time he had recognized his wife Edna, and had known that the younger woman was his daughter Angelica. But they were only types, shadows of the wisdom that was to come. Now he also knew Sophia, the embodiment of God's Holy Wisdom on Earth. He almost had his life back, but the past seemed empty and without meaning. He intended to make the future worth something. His opera had to open people's eyes to the truth about the black iron prison in which they lived, a malevolent illusion imposed upon them by mysterious dark forces whose goals were power and control.

When the doorbell rang, he got up and opened the front door, something that never would have occurred to him just yesterday. It was his daughter, and she had a young man with her.

"Dad," she bubbled. "I want you to meet Bobby, my fiancé."

The young man looked familiar, a handsome, dark-haired youth with the fire of life in his eyes. He looked good enough for Angelica, but Rob studied him carefully to make sure that he didn't have reptilian eyes.

They sat down in the dining area and shared coffee and conversation. Angelica was pleased that her father appeared to be doing so well. When they first brought him home from the hospital, he had seemed like a zombie. Now he had the old twinkle back in his blue eyes.

"What do you do for a living?" Rob asked.

"I'm a student," Bobby said. "My major is archaeology. And I have a part-time job at the museum."

"He's next in line to be assistant curator," Angelica added. "As soon as he graduates."

Rob nodded. He asked the questions that were expected of him, the same questions that Edna's father had asked of him, many years ago. That interview hadn't gone so well, but this one seemed pleasant, although a bit awkward. He was beginning to like the young man. He seemed familiar, like somebody out of a dream that he once had.

"Dad,: Angelica said, "the reason I came here today was to ask you to give me away. As the father of the bride. If you're well enough, that is."

"Of course I'm well enough. If I have to get someone to push me down the aisle in a wheelchair, I'll be there."

Angelica burst out in tears of joy. "Oh, I'm so happy!" she managed to choke out.

"So when is the wedding? Have you set a date?"

"Well," Bobby said, "we have to coordinate with my best man. Actually, Sir, we're co-best men. It's going to be a double wedding."

Angelica added, "Bobby's best friend Teddy is marrying my best friend Candy. It's going to be so wonderful, all four of us together on the same day!"

It wasn't until that night, while he lay in bed awake with Edna snoring lightly beside him, that Robert Wells realized that he had dreamed of Bobby and Teddy, and Candy, but not Angelica. The girl in his dream had a different name. Still, the coincidence was eerie and inexplicable. Perhaps he could make use of this new information for his opera. A love story certainly would make it more interesting to the audience. Ah, yes, Lorelei / Sophia. Well, in the opera he'd call her Sophia, to clue the audience in to the fact that Holy Wisdom was here on Earth and trying to help them see the Truth. The rest of the message, the core Truth, would lie in the music, not the words, but the pure tonal vibrations.

#

The homeless shelter went dark at night. They called it lights out, when all of the men who were not residents must leave and all who were residents must go to sleep in the twelve-bed dormitory. The implant realized that it was dying – not only its batteries, but its life force was ebbing away. It had left the new host in hopes of finding a better prospect, one with more stable mental faculties, but now it realized that it had no time for that. With the last of its strength, it crawled across the faces of the sleeping men and laid its eggs in their eyes. The children would know what to do; they would carry its genetic memory. Its final labor completed, it crawled up the wall and stuck itself onto the plaster ceiling, near the light fixture, where it felt warm.

Before the day broke, two big men in black suits picked the lock on the front door, came in with flashlights and deployed their detection devices. The implant didn't realize that they were searching for it, but it did sense that they had evil intentions. With the last bit of its waning strength, it dropped its final few eggs onto their heads. They began rubbing their eyes.

"My eyes itch," one of them whispered.

"Mine, too," the other one said. "Must be dust or something falling from the ceiling."

Then, losing its grip on the ceiling, the implant fell to the floor at their feet.

One of the men took a pair of tweezers out of his pocket, picked up the device and dropped it into a glass bottle, screwed the lid on tight and stashed it in his pocket.

One of the sleepers began to stir, mumbling something incomprehensible, then tossing the blanket aside and rolling over. Fearing discovery, the two men in black stopped talking and tiptoed out of the dormitory. They left the shelter unseen by human eyes and drove back to their headquarters with the device. Messenger Josiah would be pleased.

#

In the inner sanctum of the Church of the Unknown God, Father Diep performed his private supplication on behalf of the congregation and Robert Wells. He sensed that the Seed of Salvation had been planted in the soil of Berkeley, California, and that it needed the water of prayer to help it germinate and grow.

New life had entered the lives of ordinary people; he could see it in their eyes when he walked down the street, when he bought groceries or waited for a bus. Where just a few weeks ago they had passed him by without seeming to notice, total strangers smiled and waved, sometimes even said hello to the priest in his black vestments. It was as if they had awakened from a dream.

#

In a secret laboratory in the basement of the Alliance Software building, technicians probed the dead implant to discover its secrets. This cybernetic organism resembled a common banana slug, but it contained a computer chip and lithium batteries. Studying the MRI of this alien creature, they placed it under the lighted magnifying lens, sliced it open along the meridian and extracted the computer chip. The operation was bloodless, since the biological organism was quite dead. Half expecting to see the Intel logo, they examined the chip under a scanning electron microscope.

Messenger Josiah, not content with the retrieval of the device, desired to know how it worked, what it was made of and how the Agency might duplicate the device for its own purposes. The world around them was beginning to change. Chaos had entered where order used to prevail.

#

Robert Wells stood nervously behind the podium, while the college students and professors of music seated in the darkened auditorium politely clapped. He cleared his throat, shuffled his papers and began the presentation of his first speech on the art and craft of music.

"First, music is magic. Not magical, but magic, pure and simple. The old saying that music soothes the savage breast is wiser and more true than you might think. The rhythms, cadences and tones of music affect our emotions on a deep level, an they can also guide our thoughts, in either a positive or a negative direction. The polarity of the music can improve our lives or wound us, carry us to the heights of ecstasy or bury us in sorrow.

Music, at its core, is organized sound. We form music by the vibration of a string, or a reed, or some other device, which in turns sets the air into a sympathetic vibration, which in turn sets your inner ear into a sympathetic vibration. The magic lies in the fact that our world is made up of sympathetic vibrations, and we do not know the source of the original vibration which has set all of these sympathetic vibrations into motion."

Rob couldn't see the audience in the darkness beyond the stage, which was a good thing, since about half of them wore blank stares of incomprehension, while the other half began to doze off. He continued:

"The beat, or metric of a musical composition may seek to simulate a biological timer such as the heartbeat, or it may seek to change the biorhythms of the listener to match a new and innovative metric. When a piece of music is sung, the listeners respond most strongly to clear, open vowels. The consonants merely provide punctuation to the vowels. As such, the consonants create the metric."

Here he was moving closer to the core studies, the curriculum with which the students were familiar, so those he had not entirely lost began to perk up and pay attention. He recited the portions of his speech that he clearly remembered, referring to the written text when he faltered. He discussed Gregorian chants, which some people find totally irritating, while others find them soothing and refreshing. He discussed the major and minor modes of liturgical music, the 12-tone scale, the singing of whales and the cacophony of rap. He explained how music could make a happy person sad or lift a depressed person into an elevated state. He proposed that the right kind of music could cure cancer, as well as mental illness. He also suggested that chord changes could transform an object, such as changing your old Ford into a brand new BMW, or trading a twenty-room mansion for a two-bedroom apartment. .

"So in conclusion, Pythagoras was literally correct when he said that the universe is made of numbers, and those numbers were the music of the spheres."

The students applauded politely, quietly, even though most of them were pleased only that the ordeal had come to an end. They thought the speaker mad and his speech nonsense. The Dean of Music who had introduced Rob to the audience called for questions, but only one student raised his hand. The others were hurriedly leaving, no doubt hurrying to classes or to the cafeteria.

"How," asked the student, "can you expect us to believe in magic? Isn't that a retrograde notion from our primitive past?"

Rob smiled and said, "I believe in you." The student turned and walked away, shrugging his shoulders in disgust or frustration, Rob wasn't sure which. He had expected the students at UC Berkeley to be more open-minded. After all, the University was the home of radical politics and social experimentation. The disappointment was not all on his side.

As he walked through the parking lot to the bus stop for a ride home, he felt infinitely rejected and dejected. The bench was already occupied by three women with their shopping bags full of groceries, so he stood nearby and looked down the street to see whether a bus was coming. There, not more than fifty feet away, was the old derelict with his cardboard sign.   It read in clumsy, hand-drawn lettering:

MUSIC IS MAGIC, MUSIC HEALS ALL ILLS.

On impulse, without giving it any thought, Rob ran down the street and grabbed the derelict in a bear hug. They were kindred souls, distributing the same message through different media.

He thought that this should be the justification of his entire life, a moment of pure innocent bliss, but the derelict pushed him away.

"Stop it, man, you're bending my sign!"

#

Edna Eileen Stax Wells began writing in her notebook, a triple-clasp, blue cloth notebook filled with blank paper. "Time," she began, "is fungible." She thought for a moment, chewing on the end of her ballpoint pen, then wrote further, "Memory is also fungible. Both can be exchanged for other commodities of equal or similar value. Not only are time and space dimensions of space-time, but the third component of memory must be added to form space-time-memory. We spend our lives from birth in a certain order, unless something happens to upset the order, the symmetry, the schedule of time."

She paused to think for a moment, and then she added, "The macrocosm does not exist until someone witnesses it, solidifying the actual out of the sea of possibilities. This Heisenberg/James event of witnessing is a quantum jump."

She put down the pen and took a sip of coffee. It had grown cold sitting in the ceramic mug on her desk. She didn't care. The cold coffee was simply a sign of the entropy that was overtaking her, overtaking them all, as the light began to darken.

Outside in the night, a raccoon clawed at the window, wanting to come inside.

#####

REFERENCES

Angus, S. *The Mystery-Religions*. New York: Dover Publications, Inc., 1928, 1975.

De Santillana, Giorgio, and Hertha Von Dechend, *Hamlet's Mill*. Jaffrey, New Hampshire: David R. Godine, Publisher, Inc., 1977.

Graves, Robert. *The Greek Myths*. London: The Folio Society, 1955, 1957, 1960, 1996.

Horn, Thomas. *Apollyon Rising 2012: The Lost Symbol Found and the Final Mystery of the Great Seal Revealed*. Defender, 2009.

Martin, Malachi. *Hostage to the Devil: The Possession and Exorcism of Five Contemporary Americans*. New York: Harper, 1992.

Meyer, Marvin W., and Richard Smith, Eds. *Ancient Christian Magic: Coptic Texts of Ritual Power*. Princeton University Press, 1994, 1999.

Missler, Chuck. *Cosmic Codes: Hidden Messages from the Edge of Eternity*. Coeur d'Alene, ID: Koinonia House, 1999.

Peake, Anthony. *The Daemon: A Guide to Your Extraordinary Secret Self*. London: Arcturus, 2008.

Shuré, Edouard. *Pythagoras and the Delphic Mysteries*. 1906. At sacredtexts.com

Stapp, Henry P. *Mind, Matter, and Quantum Mechanics*. New York: Springer-Verlag, 1993.

Trzaskoma, Stephen M., R. Scott Smith, and Stephen Brunet. *Anthology of Classical Myth: Primary Sources in Translation*. Indianapolis / Cambridge: Hackett Publishing Company, Inc., 2004.

Lovingly crafted by Philip K. Dick's wife Tessa B. Dick, this novel delivers the surreal world of madness that blends into sanity. The story demonstrates a deep love for the characters who must wander through the maze which keeps them trapped in illusion. They strive to make sense of their world, only to find that reality changes every time they think that they understand it. This mind-opening adventure will take you through the alternate worlds required by quantum physics, the psychology of William James and the prison that our world has become.

~~~

Other books by Tessa B. Dick

Origins Part One: Thor's Hammer, a novel based on the story of Genesis 6 and the evidence presented in Michael Cremo's *Forbidden Archaeology*, blended with Richard Hoagland's assertion that "We are the Martians."

Allegro's Mushroom, an exegesis of the controversial book outlining John Allegro's theory that Judeo-Christian religion is based on an ancient mushroom cult.

Tessa B. Dick: My Life on the Edge of Reality, a memoir about the author's childhood experience, including participation in a government-sponsored experiment in mind control.

Philip K. Dick: Remembering Firebright, a memoir recalling the astonishing spiritual experiences that the author shared with her husband.

~~~~~

Printed in Great Britain
by Amazon

35784794R00139